UNFORGETTABLE

"Mind if I ask you a personal question?" Marcel asked.

"Yes."

"All right, I'll ask it anyway."

"Surprise, surprise."

"Is there anyone special in your life?"

Diana's eyes flew open as she lowered the compress. "I fail to see how that's any of your business." She sat up.

Marcel followed suit. "I realize I'm prying."

"But?"

"There's no but. I'm just curious. Seems to me any man would be happy to have you."

"I'm leaving."

Before she could pull away, Marcel's electrifying touch restrained her. "Look, I'm sorry. You're right. None of this is any of my business."

It wasn't the words so much as the tone that kept her frozen on the bed. Frankly, she didn't think he was sorry at all, but his underlying and seductive baritone instantly caused her pulse to quicken and her head to fill with erotic images.

BOOK YOUR PLACE ON OUR WEBSITE AND MAKE THE ARABESQUE ROMANCE CONNECTION!

We've created a customized website just for our very special Arabesque readers, where you can get the inside scoop on everything that's going on with Arabesque romance novels.

When you come online, you'll have the exciting opportunity to:

- View covers of upcoming books

- Learn about our future publishing schedule (listed by publication month and author)

- Find out when your favorite authors will be visiting a city near you

- Search for and order backlist books

- Check out author bios and background information

- Send e-mail to your favorite authors

- Join us in weekly chats with authors, readers and other guests

- Get writing guidelines

- AND MUCH MORE!

Visit our website at
http://www.arabesquebooks.com

UNFORGETTABLE

ADRIANNE BYRD

BET Publications, LLC
http://www.bet.com
http://www.arabesquebooks.com

Prologue

"Casanova Brown is getting married?" Astonishment widened Ophelia Missler's beautiful eyes. "It's a miracle. Did anyone call the Seven Hundred Club?"

"No one's more surprised than I am." Solomon chuckled and reached for his coffee.

Silence fell between the two friends nestled around a small table in the corner of Joe Mugg's, their favorite coffee shop in downtown Atlanta.

Finally, Ophelia's gaze narrowed as her full lips twitched at the corners. "Is this woman pregnant or something?"

A small smile lingered on Solomon Bassett's lips. "Not that I'm aware of."

"Is she blackmailing him?"

His smile broadened. "No." He sipped his coffee.

Another silence lapsed before a question tumbled forth. "Has anyone given him a drug test?"

Solomon nearly spewed out his coffee, but managed to swallow and shake his head. "I hadn't thought of that."

She rolled her eyes as if to say, *Well, there you go.*

"I'm fairly positive he hasn't been drugged. He's way too happy about all of this." Solomon leaned back in his chair as his gaze surveyed the coffee shop and caught a few male stares cast in their direction. That wasn't unusual. Ophelia was a beautiful woman with a perfect honey-coated complexion and eyes the color of topaz. Her thick, sandy brown hair held streaks of blond and hung in tight ringlets past her shoulders.

To stare at her was to be mesmerized and Solomon had been under her spell for twenty-one years and counting.

"Well, I don't believe it," Ophelia said, shaking her head. "Drugs give people the illusion of being happy. I've worked in a rehabilitation center for ten years. I ought to know."

Solomon laughed as his long fingers reached for his cup again. "You're in shock."

"Damn right. I'm surprised that you're not."

"Trust me, I was—the moment he walked into my office with stars in his eyes claiming to have found his match."

Ophelia's delicate brows arched. "His match?"

He nodded. "A challenge—or maybe I should say a mystery."

She frowned and set her mug down. "Okay. You've piqued my curiosity. Who's the lucky woman? And how come I wasn't told sooner about this great love of Casanova's life?"

He hesitated. It was hard for Solomon to discern if he detected jealousy in her voice. Growing up, Solomon, Ophelia, and Marcel, nicknamed Casanova Brown by close friends, were like the three musketeers. They were the best of friends, yet still had a few secrets weaved between them.

Solomon first met Marcel when his family moved in next door to him in the summer of '78. Their love of sports was all it took to seal their lifelong friendship. It was the year when Reggie Jackson, O.J. Simpson, Muhammad Ali, and Kareem Abdul Jabbar ruled their world. Solomon and Marcel vowed to be the first athletes to win the Super Bowl, the NBA finals, and World Series. Life was good.

In the winter of '81, a scrawny girl, who they originally suspected had cooties, wormed her way into their private club. It was hard to ignore her. She could sail a fastball past the best players in the neighborhood and could run like the wind. Life was better.

By the time puberty hit, Ophelia's long, thin legs suddenly had shape to them and her round bottom was a nice distraction in Gloria Vanderbilt jeans. And Lord, her breasts. Solomon, to this day, didn't know where they came from, but suddenly she had them and the best pair in their junior high school. His brotherly affection toward her changed overnight and life had never been the same.

Solomon never found the words to tell Ophelia about his feelings mainly because she always seemed more attracted to Marcel. How could he blame her? Most women were drawn to Casanova and a lot of men wanted to *be* him . . . including Solomon.

Who wouldn't want to be a six-four brick house with enough smoothness to melt the thickest iceberg around any woman's heart?

Ophelia waved a hand in front of him. "Earth to Solomon."

He laughed. "Oh, sorry."

"Maybe I should be asking whether you're on drugs. You keep zoning out on me."

"Hardly."

"Well?" Her brows arched high. "Who's the lucky woman?"

"If Marcel hasn't told you, then maybe I should wait until you get the invitation. Let it be a surprise."

"A surprise?" She leaned back in her chair. "It's too late for that. Why don't you just tell me the story?"

"I think Marcel should tell this one."

"Marcel isn't here. So spill it."

Solomon hesitated.

Ophelia placed her arms on the table and leaned forward and locked gazes with her magnetic golden orbs. "We're supposed to be able to tell each other everything, remember?"

He was nodding before he realized it and in the next second he told the story of how Casanova Brown found his true love. . . .

In need of
a change

One

nine months ago

Marcel Taylor believed there was no better way to start the day than surrounded by gorgeous women, which was why the fairer sex made up 92 percent of the employees at T&B Entertainment. And not just model types, though they worked there too, but all types of women. Tall, short, thick, or full-figured; Marcel loved them all.

At thirty-five, he'd spent three-quarters of his life probing, discovering, enjoying, and reveling in what he'd termed "the essence of a woman." Anyone who laughed at the expression truly didn't know or understand them.

Now as he sat poised at the head of the conference table, a pair of long, shapely caramel-colored legs caught and held his attention. As they slowly crossed, a languid smile caressed his lips. His brows hiked as a beautifully manicured hand glided up her calf to midthigh.

"Mr. Taylor?"

Solomon wrangled Marcel's runaway thoughts. "Yes?" He straightened in his chair and turned toward his colleague and best friend.

Solomon Bassett's face twisted into a frown. "And on that note, I think we're done."

Having been caught daydreaming, Marcel managed a lopsided grin. "No argument here."

Nora Gibson's eyes twinkled with amusement as she slowly uncrossed her legs—the source of Marcel's distraction.

The rest of the associates, one man and seven women, huddled around the long conference table quickly closed their briefcases and collected their things.

Solomon's lips hung on to their frown as he shook his head. "My presentation bored you?" he asked just low enough for Marcel's ears.

"I heard every word," Marcel affirmed with honesty.

"Except my joke at the end."

"It was a bad joke."

Solomon's mouth wrestled into a balmy smile. "I screwed up the punch line, didn't I?"

"As always." Marcel chuckled and slapped his hand against his friend's back. "But don't worry. I haven't given up on you. One day, you'll get it right."

Solomon shook his head. "That's good to know."

One on one, Solomon was an easygoing and funny guy, but put him in front of a crowd or small group and he was transformed into this awkward, almost geeky persona.

"What did you think about that new girl group Selena wants to sign?"

Marcel shook his head. "What kind of name is 2Juicy?"

"They'll definitely have to get rid of that name. And put on a little more clothing."

"Now let's not be too hasty," Marcel deadpanned. "They do have incredible bodies."

Solomon rolled his eyes. "I know that skin is in, but they need a little more than thongs and breast pasties, don't you think?"

Nora's syrupy voice dripped into their conversation. "I know my two cents might not count for much, but I like them."

The men turned and focused their attention on the approaching caramel beauty.

Marcel met her eyes. "Is that right? What do you like about them?"

"Well," she said, crossing her arms, "they have good stage presence and they write all their own material."

"Being naked on the stage isn't good stage presence," Solomon said, cocking his head.

"They grab the audience's attention, which is what's important."

"She has a good point," Marcel intoned. "But," he added, "I also have to agree with Solomon. They might be a little *too* over the top. If they rework their image and come up with some better material— something that makes them stand out from the other underdressed groups—I'll take another look at them."

Her eyes twinkled. "You're the boss."

Solomon groaned from beside them and then moved toward the door.

Marcel looked up. "Wait. I'll come with you. I need to talk to you about next weekend."

"Mr. Taylor." Nora stopped him before he could walk away. "Are we still crunching numbers over lunch?"

He hesitated before answering. "Not today. I have some other pressing matters I have to attend to. Just leave the numbers with Diana and I'll go over them later."

For a millisecond, disappointment, irritation, and annoyance rippled across her face before she forced a smile. "Certainly." A strange and awkward moment passed before she turned and walked away.

"Are you feeling all right?" Solomon asked, staring at him.

Marcel opened his mouth ready to confess that everything wasn't okay. Though as close as they were and despite the many things they'd shared together, he wasn't ready to burden Solomon with his troubles. "I'm fine."

His friend's frown deepened.

"Really," Marcel assured him.

"Then excuse my shock," Solomon said, leading the way out of the conference room. "But I've never known Casanova Brown to brush off the attention of a beautiful woman, especially one who wants to 'crunch' numbers over lunch."

Marcel shrugged. "One should never mix business with pleasure."

"So you keep saying."

Breezing into Solomon's office, Marcel closed the door behind them. "About the ball next month—"

Solomon clapped and rubbed his hands together as his eyes became as wide as silver dollars with excitement. "We're going to have a blast. Our first masquerade ball—a singles party at that."

Marcel's excitement didn't match his friend's. "It's just a costume party."

"Hey, no one throws a party like my uncle Willy," Solomon continued. "According to him, the women will outnumber the men four to one. We'll be like kids in a candy shop. Did you get a chance to read the rules?" Solomon dropped into his chair.

"I glanced at them. Why aren't we allowed to remove our masks or give out our real names?"

"To heighten the excitement and to give everything a mysterious flare. I personally like it. I'm going to be either Don Juan de Marco or Zorro. What do you think?"

"Please, don't ask me." Marcel lowered onto the plush sofa across from the bar and tilted his head back. "I'm not sure I'm going to make it."

"You're joking." Solomon's voice held a note of alarm. "You have to come. I've already promised Uncle Willy."

Marcel exhaled in attempt to ward off the anxiety of others' expectations. "The last thing I need in my life is another party where I meet the same type of women: gorgeous on the outside but empty on the inside."

When a rush of silence followed his statement, he peeked over at Solomon's desk to make sure he was still in the room.

His friend stared as though he'd never seen Marcel before.

"All right. Out with it. What's bothering you?"

"Nothing." He shifted uncomfortably and then stared up at the ceiling. "I think I need a vacation."

"From work?"

"From everything," he confessed, feeling a ripple of relief after finally telling someone. "I need a change. I'm tired of dealing with shady industry people, artists' attitudes, traveling around the globe, and then having nothing to show for it."

Solomon shared a half laugh. "Nothing to show for it? What are you talking about? We run one of the top labels in the music industry. We accomplished everything we set out to do. We have several homes, cars—"

Marcel interrupted him. "Everything that doesn't mean a damn thing. At least nothing that's going to matter in the end."

Solomon gaped.

"Come on." Marcel turned to catch his gaze. "What would you give up to win Ophelia's heart—marry her even?"

"I, uh . . ."

Marcel laughed at the instant darkening of his friend's complexion. "Relax. It's not like she just walked into the room."

Solomon swallowed and then got up from his desk. "What's your point?" he asked, as he headed over to the bar.

"My point is I want what you have."

"What—to be considered nothing more than a brother to a woman you're in love with?" Solomon reached for the bottle of scotch. "If so, then you're more screwed up in the head than I thought. Drink?"

Marcel waved off the offer, but stood up to join him. "Okay. Maybe not exactly what you have. But, at least you know *who* you want. Not to mention, Ophelia is a fine woman. She's beautiful, smart, independent—"

"You're not about to tell me you're in love with

her too, are you?" Solomon tossed back a shot and then frowned through the burn.

"No." Marcel shook his head, ignoring the memory of once having a crush on the golden-eyed beauty. "I would never do you like that."

Relief shrank Solomon's shoulders. "Well, that's good to know." He capped the bottle. "So where does this leave us?"

"Restless," Marcel mumbled. "Bored."

"I can't believe my ears. Casa—"

"Please, stop calling me that."

Solomon held up his hands in surrender. "O-okay."

Marcel shrugged. "Don't you ever get tired of it all?"

"With the job or with women?"

"Both."

Solomon laughed. "The job . . . sometimes. Women . . . can't say that I have. Course, I don't pull in the numbers you do."

"I need time off to myself." Marcel gazed at an amber bottle of alcohol while his thoughts ambled restlessly. "If I told you something, would you laugh?"

"I'll try not to."

"I'm thinking about settling down." He refused to look up during the long silence, but plunged ahead. "One woman—to have and to hold till death do us part. That kind of thing. Like our parents."

"Hey, I have something you might want to check out," Solomon said.

Marcel's gaze crept up when a card was thrust in front of him to read. "Dr. Michael Porter? You think I need a shrink?"

"It couldn't hurt."

They stared at each other.

"Look," Solomon began. "As much as I believe in the sanctity of marriage, I also believe that the institution isn't meant for everyone, especially someone with your track record. Let's face it, you bore easily."

"Fine." He finally grabbed the card and pocketed it. "A lot of good it will do."

A hard knock sounded at the door and the men barely had enough time to look up before Diana Guy stuck her head through the door.

"There you are," she said, locking gazes with Marcel and sliding her thick, black-wire-frame glasses up her slender nose. "Your father is waiting for you in your office."

Marcel straightened. "What's *he* doing here?" he asked, moving toward the door.

"I don't know, but he doesn't look too happy."

"Nothing new there," Solomon chimed, following his partner through the doorway. "Surely, he's not here because of the profit reports. We're up a full twelve percent."

Marcel shook his head as he strode down the hallway taking long strides. "I swear I regret more and more every day asking him to invest in this company. His constant interference is going to drive me to an early grave."

Solomon laughed. "Maybe we can arrange it so we can get our plots next to each other."

Opening his office door, Marcel gestured for Solomon to go first.

"Gee, thanks," Solomon mumbled under his breath as he entered.

Diana returned to her desk outside his office.

"Five minutes," he instructed.

She gave him a curt nod.

Marcel turned and entered his office with a broad, plastic smile. "Pop, what a pleasure to see you."

Donald Taylor stood from his chair. His extra two inches of height easily gave him the physical dominance he loved to lord over his son. "Marcel," he said with a slight nod. "I hope I'm not interrupting your business schedule."

"Of course not. You're welcome any time."

"Well," Donald said, glancing over at Solomon, "I'm not here on business." He paused as if waiting for his meaning to sink in, but when it didn't he looked back at his son. "I was wondering if I could talk to you for a few minutes."

Marcel nodded. "Yes, of course."

Solomon remained mute while holding his painted-on smile.

"*Alone,*" Donald added with another glance at Solomon.

"Oh," Solomon said, finally emerging from his stupor, and blinked with embarrassment. "Gotcha."

Marcel managed to suppress a laugh at Solomon's hasty exit, and then glanced at his watch as he made his way around the desk. "Okay, now that you've cleared the room, what can I do for you?" He eased into his chair.

His father drew in a deep breath. "How much time do I have before Diana comes in here to excuse you to a nonexisting emergency meeting?"

The men locked gazes, before Marcel answered with brutal honesty. "Two minutes."

"Then I'll get right to the point." He erected his tall frame and blurted the news. "Your mother and I are getting a divorce."

Two

Diana stared at her letter of resignation on her computer screen but lacked the guts to print out the damn thing. Quitting would be the right thing to do, the voice in her head assured her. A person with her education, experience, and dedication should be able to find employment anywhere.

She moved her mouse to hover over the printer icon.

The other rational voice in her head cut in to stop her. *Don't be stupid. You can't afford to quit. Have you forgotten about the stack of medical bills for your grandmother?* Despair overwhelmed her as a list of responsibilities ran through her mind. *You can't quit until you find another job first.*

Resolute, Diana closed the document, checked her watch, and stood up from her cluttered desk.

Marcel Taylor wasn't difficult to work with—on the contrary. Despite his image as a ladies' man, Taylor was as competent as he was charming, intelligent as he was handsome. In her opinion, her employer was the total package: wealthy, attractive, smart, attractive, charismatic, and attractive.

She shook her head and cleared her thoughts. Every woman at T&B Entertainment coveted the handsome president. With so many beautiful women adoring him, Mr. Taylor never noticed his plain Jane secretary, Diana.

At Marcel's door, she took in a deep breath, knocked, and entered. "Mr. Taylor . . ."

She stopped cold at her boss's stunned expression and then glanced uncertainly at Donald Taylor, equally floored to see unguarded emotions on the older man's usual stoic face.

Marcel cleared his throat. "Diana, cancel whatever it is."

"Yes, sir." Her gaze swept over him a final time before she backed out of the office. After the door clicked behind her, she replayed the scene in her mind. *Something's going on,* she thought, returning to her desk. *Something big.*

"Ahem."

Diana looked up at the always-stylish Nora grinning down at her with a stack of papers. "Can I help you?"

Nora's coral-colored lips beamed wider. "As a matter of fact, you can. Marcel instructed me to leave these figures with you." Unceremoniously, she plopped the mound of paper onto the desk. "By the way," she said, moving toward his office door. "Is he in now?"

"Wait." Diana stopped Nora before her hand landed on the doorknob. "He's in an important meeting right now."

"With who?"

Diana's brows arched, her expression clearly saying, *That's none of your business.*

Nora turned from Marcel's door and settled her hands on her hips. The ex-model's pose appeared provocative with little effort.

Diana's jealousy proved hard to ignore.

"How long have they been in there?" Nora asked.

Diana stood and removed the stacked reports from her desk and placed them on top of the nearest file cabinet. A few of the items on the top page, however, caught her attention and she lifted the top sheet. "My goodness."

"I know, I know." Nora rolled her eyes. "We're a little over budget. But it's not like we're not going to recoup the money from Belinda's CD sales."

"It's her first CD. There's no guarantee that we're going to recoup much of anything," Diana said, now picking up the second sheet. "There's no way Mr. Taylor is going to approve most of this stuff. Why does she need a top-of-the-line tour bus? She's only scheduled to do eight cities."

"It never hurts to ask for things. The most Marcel can say is no."

Diana placed the papers back and shook her head while she returned to her desk. It wasn't the first time she wondered how Nora got her job. The woman had no experience in the music industry, she constantly put her nose in places it didn't belong, and she made it her business to know where and what the president was doing at all times.

"Any idea what they're discussing?" Nora's attention had drifted back to Taylor's closed door.

Diana glanced at Nora, her irritation just barely

concealed. "He canceled your lunch meeting. Did he not tell you?"

"Oh, yes. He told me. I'm curious to know what was so important he had to cancel our date—I mean, our appointment."

"I don't know."

Nora's arched brows rose. "I find that hard to believe, Ms. *Efficient*. I bet you know everything that goes on in Marcel's life." She moved back toward Diana's desk. "Am I right?"

Diana sighed at the woman's diva theatrics. "Ms. Gibson, I wouldn't be good at my job if I betrayed Mr. Taylor's confidence. Now, would I?"

Nora's cinnamon gaze raked over Diana, making her self-conscious of her drab clothes and her dowdy, pinned-back hairstyle. Chin high, she reached for the first thing in her in-box.

Nora sashayed to the front of her desk, leaned her hip against it, and crossed her arms. "I've only been here a few months. I don't mean to step on anyone's toes, especially yours. I know Marcel thinks the world of you."

Diana cringed at the familiarity with which Nora said his name and looked up. "Let me guess: you want us to be friends?"

Irritation flashed behind the beautiful woman's eyes and then disappeared. "Why, yes."

A smile on her face, Diana's hands now zoomed across her keyboard.

"What's so funny?" Nora asked.

"Nothing. It's just that I've had this same conversation with more than half the women working here. I'm going to tell you what I told them: if your attraction to Mr. Taylor is going to hinder you from doing your job, then maybe you should consider seeking employment elsewhere. He has a strict rule about office romances with employees: he doesn't do it."

Nora pushed away from the desk, but Diana was saved when Marcel's office door jerked open and Donald Taylor rushed out.

In the few seconds it took for him to pass by, Diana caught the same look of anguish chiseled in his strong features.

"Diana," Taylor called. "Could you come in here?"

She jumped at his gruff voice and quickly grabbed a pen and notepad.

"Well, something's going on," Nora said.

Diana ignored her and hurried into Taylor's office. Once inside, she closed the door behind her, and then glanced around to find her boss by the window.

She eased into a leather chair and waited as he stared out at the city view.

Long seconds ticked into awkward minutes and still she waited. During the silence, she used the time to study his incredible profile.

Working in the entertainment business, Diana had certainly seen her share of flashy and suave dressers, but no one filled out a suit or commanded attention like Mr. Taylor.

He turned suddenly and caught her gaze. Flustered, she imprisoned every ounce of air that her lungs could hold until he looked away.

"Are your parents still together?" he asked.

Diana blanched, caught off guard by such a personal question. She answered in a low voice, "My mother passed away when I was ten."

Sympathy softened his gaze. "I'm sorry to hear that."

"It was a long time ago," she said, dropping her gaze to the blank page in her notepad. The silence heightened to a deafening decibel but she refused to look up again.

"Did your father ever remarry?"

Briefly, she thought about not answering. After all, it wasn't any of his business, but in the end the truth spilled out.

"My parents were never married."

Another long silence lapsed.

"I'm sorry. I shouldn't have asked."

She chanced a look up and found he'd turned back toward the window. "Is something wrong?"

He was quiet for so long, she assumed he wouldn't answer.

"Yes and no," he finally said, moving away from the window and over to his desk. "I need you to help me with something."

"Of course, sir."

Once he was settled into his chair, their gazes locked once again. "This matter is not to be discussed with anyone . . . including Mr. Bassett."

Startled and then curious, Diana nodded. "Yes, sir."

Beneath his leveled gaze, a strange and delicious warmth spread throughout her body.

"I need you to help me find my mother."

The sentence rolled over her head. "Excuse me?"

Marcel shifted in his chair. "Um, my parents are . . . separated—at the moment." He reached for a folded piece of paper from the corner of his desk. "She left a note."

"A note?" she repeated, trying to follow the conversation.

"Yeah." He drew in a deep breath. "She asked my

father not to try and find her because she needs some time to think."

In the two years Diana had worked for Marcel, it wasn't uncommon for her to lend a hand in his personal life as well as his professional. Those services usually included sending flowers or candy, or purchasing concert tickets and arranging shopping sprees. This was something else entirely.

"I'm not quite sure I'm the one who—"

He held up the letter. "You're perfect."

She frowned. *How long have I been waiting to hear that?*

"According to this she's going somewhere in Italy," he continued. "Since she's always talked about visiting Venice, I think we should start there."

"But if Camille doesn't want to be found—"

Marcel held up a finger. "Actually, she said she doesn't want my father to find her. I'm not my father."

"Then maybe you should wait until Camille tries to contact you." It was the wrong thing to say.

His lips thinned into a straight line. "I don't want to wait. Can you do this for me?"

Again their eyes met and Diana pretended her skin didn't tingle and her breath hadn't hitched, but this time she was the first to look away. "Consider it done." She stood from her chair.

When she moved toward the door, he moved with her.

"Diana."

She turned, surprised to find him standing so close. "Do me a favor and don't tell anyone about this."

She smiled. "Don't worry. I know how to keep a secret."

Three

Marcel closed the door and drew in an unsteady breath. *Diana to the rescue.* At least he found comfort in his reliable secretary. Lord knows, she could find a needle in a haystack let alone a little old black woman in Venice, Italy. What would he do if Diana weren't around?

The woman had a way of making him look good. Maybe he should do something for her—send her on a trip or something. He thought for a moment and couldn't remember whether in the past two years she'd ever taken a vacation or even called in sick.

He frowned. Surely, he was mistaken.

Shaking off the thought, he promised himself to look into it later. Right now, he needed to figure out what to do about his parents.

The news of their possible divorce rattled him like nothing before. More questions than answers plagued him. As usual his father was vague with details, but Donald Taylor kept many things close to his vest.

Instead of returning to his desk, Marcel detoured to the leather sofa at the opposite end and stretched out. Who'd ever heard of getting a divorce after forty years of marriage?

He groaned, closed his eyes, and massaged his temples. For as long as he could remember, his parents, despite their night-and-day personalities, were happy. However, Marcel suspected the real problem was his father's retirement.

A year ago, dear old Dad retired from the law firm of Hughes, Taylor & Hughes and invaded his mother's peaceful world of music and quiet social functions. The man of the house was home and he wanted his wonderful wife to devote all her precious time to him. This undoubtedly drove her crazy.

The last time Marcel talked with her, she wanted his father to take up golf—a nice sport that took hours to play.

It was a bad idea.

Donald Taylor, a frugal man, couldn't see the point in spending so much money to chase a small ball around acres of grass.

Marcel's mother's need for time was likely code for: she wanted a vacation from her husband. Now his father tossed the word *divorce* around more as a threat than anything else—at least he hoped.

A quick knock jarred Marcel from his thoughts, but before he answered, Solomon poked his head inside.

"Is the coast clear?"

"All clear." Marcel sat up and erased the worry from his face.

"Good," Solomon answered. "Looks like you survived the surprise attack. Any bombs I should know about?"

"Nah. Just family stuff."

Solomon nodded and entered the room proudly presenting a magazine to Marcel. "Look who's on the cover of *Rolling Stone.*"

Marcel stared at his picture. A red and white cape donned his shoulders while an oversize gold crown adorned his head. At the bottom in large block letters the cover line asked the question: THE NEW PRINCE OF HIP-HOP?

"Wow," he said.

"Is that all you can say?" Solomon smiled and flipped the cover around so he could read it again. "You're off the charts, man."

Suddenly, the first eight notes of "Superfly" filled the room and Marcel dug into his pocket and retrieved his pager. "It's Tee Bo. Are we still passing through Club Secrets tonight?"

"Wouldn't miss it. That cat from WZEZ radio station is deejaying. Word is he's off the chain."

"Cool." Marcel typed in his answer and then pocketed the device. "If we're going, then I need to head over to the house and work on a few things first and feed Brandy." It wasn't the whole truth, but it was a good enough excuse to leave the office.

After gathering his things, Solomon walked Marcel out of his office, continuing to talk to him through the halls and over to the elevator bay. Marcel couldn't concentrate and resigned himself to just smile and nod.

When the elevator arrived, Solomon pounded Marcel's back. "Well, I'll catch you at the club later."

"You bet." He smiled and then stepped into the empty compartment. Thankful for the solitude, he pressed the button for the lobby.

"Hold the elevator," a voice called out a second before a slender hand jutted between the sliding doors and stopped them from closing.

When they opened again, the lovely Nora Gibson appeared. "Mind if I ride down with you?" she asked in a tone thick with seduction.

A broad smile galloped across Marcel's face at the not-so-hidden innuendo. "Of course not, Ms. Gibson."

She lit up and stepped inside and the clean scent of Glow perfume tickled his nose.

The doors closed.

"Which floor?" he asked.

"The lobby is fine." She moved closer and crowded his personal space. "You're a hard man to catch."

He stepped back. "Is that right?"

"Yeah." She stepped forward. "You know, if I didn't know better I'd think you were avoiding me."

"That's not true."

"All right. Then you're avoiding being *alone* with me."

The elevator slowed to a stop on the seventh floor.

Nora eased away as the door slid open and revealed Diana.

Marcel sighed with relief. "Diana," he said, immediately feeling guilty for doing nothing wrong. "Going down?"

Diana's gaze darted between him and Nora. For a brief second, she looked dubious about joining them.

"The lobby, please," she said, stepping inside and planting herself between them.

While a deafening silence filled the small space, Marcel chanced a side glance at his secretary. Her eyes cut away before their gazes met, and he had the distinct impression that she was angry. He frowned, disturbed by the notion.

His gaze shifted to Nora and received a wide smile and a secretive wink. He looked away and struggled not to roll his eyes, but his attention quickly returned to Diana.

"Heading out for lunch?" he asked.

She glanced at him. "Who, me?"

He smiled and rocked on the balls of his feet. "Yes, you."

"I'm taking the rest of the day off. I told you yesterday I have a few personal matters to take care of this afternoon."

"Oh." He had forgotten. "So about that project—"

"I'm already on it," she assured him.

The elevator finally arrived at its destination and Diana was the first to bolt through the doors.

He frowned as he looked after her and then followed.

"Marcel?" Nora touched his arm and reclaimed his attention. "I still need to talk with you."

"Sure. Just, uh, make an appointment with Diana. I'm sure she can get you on my schedule." He extracted his arm and moved away.

Heading out the door, Marcel realized he was rushing to catch up with Diana. A part of him wanted to clear the air about Nora. He didn't want Diana to think he'd violated his personal rule about dating women in the workplace.

He exited the tall silver and glass building, instantly relieved to find Diana standing alone out front. "Waiting for someone?"

"My ride," she answered without looking at him.

"Is something wrong with your car?"

"In the shop." She continued to be short.

"Engine trouble?"

"Brakes."

Her tone bothered him. "I can give you a lift, if you'd like."

"No, thanks." Her eyes never wavered from the driveway. Was she praying for her ride to hurry and rescue her from his company?

"Diana, is something wrong? Have I done something to upset you?"

That finally won her attention. "Sorry, I'm just a little preoccupied." Her eyes shifted from him again and a small smile hugged her lips. "There he is."

Marcel casually turned toward a black Lexus. As it coasted up the drive, he focused on the tall slender man behind the steering wheel. "Boyfriend?" he asked.

The car rolled to a stop in front of them and Diana reached for the passenger's door without answering his question.

To his surprise, the driver opened his door and got out. "You're Marcel Taylor." The man with delicate features ogled.

"I was the last time I checked." He smiled. *I would never have thought Diana liked pretty boys.*

When the driver rushed around the car to offer his hand, Marcel witnessed a flash of irritation crossing Diana's face before she crammed herself into the car.

"I'm Timothy Banks. I love T&B Records. You guys have the best acts in the biz. I've been dying to meet you ever since, well, since Di told me she worked for you." He held out his hand.

"Is that right?" Accepting the offered hand, Marcel looked down at her and found he liked the nickname. "Have you and *Di* been friends long?"

Diana glanced up from the passenger window. "Tim, we're running late."

Tim glanced at his watch. "We have plenty of time."

Her eyes hardened and glittered like polished diamonds.

Tim turned back toward Marcel with a crack smile. "We have to go."

Amused, Marcel nodded, but still wondered at the source of Diana's anger and he had no doubts that she was indeed angry. "I guess I'll see you tomorrow."

Her smile fluttered weakly as she waited for Tim to return to the driver's seat.

When the car pulled off, Marcel remained rooted by the curb reviewing everything that had just happened. Maybe he did need to do something for Diana . . . before he lost her.

Four

"What was all of that about?" Timothy asked, glancing back at Marcel through his rearview mirror.

Diana slumped against the headrest and closed her eyes. "What do you mean?"

"Are you kidding? I thought you were going to rip my head off if I didn't get back in the car. The first time I get to meet your boss and I came off looking like an idiot."

She sighed, not wanting to answer. "Sorry, but I'm on a tight schedule. That's all."

"Come on now. I'm your best friend, remember? What's going on?"

"Nothing. Can we just forget it?"

At her friend's deep breath, she expected him to continue to prod and meddle her into a confession, but instead the soft whirl of the air conditioner became the only sound between them.

The silent treatment.

"I have to look for a new job," she declared. "I can't continue to work for him."

Tim cast her a sideways glance. "Now that I've seen him in person, I don't blame you. He's gorgeous."

She sighed. "Please, not you too."

"Hey, I might be in a committed relationship, but I'm not blind to the merchandise around me."

Diana laughed and finally relaxed. "You better hope Caleb doesn't hear you talking like that."

"*You* better not tell him."

"Not as long as you make all bribes payable to Diana Guy."

Timothy shook his head. "You're a shrewd businesswoman."

"Ah, flattery. Take ten percent off your bill then." She winked.

The auto shop loomed ahead and the weight of the world settled on her shoulders. "Any guess as to how much this is going to be?"

"I thought you said they were running a special on brakes?" Timothy asked, frowning.

"Yeah, but since when does a repair estimate ever turn out to be accurate?"

"Good point." He parked the car and looked over at her. "If you need me to spot you a few, just say the word."

Diana patted his hand. "Thanks, but I should have enough."

When she went for the door, he stopped her and locked gazes. "You do know it's okay to ask for help every once in a while, don't you?"

Her answer was yes, but her pride said no. "You're a good friend, Tim." She leaned over and kissed his cheek.

He flashed her a smile. "You're not so bad your-self."

She turned and got out of the car, but as ex-pected, the repair bill was double what she'd been quoted. The explanation was the usual "we had to replace blah and blah" and "we didn't take into ac-count for such and such." Disgusted, she wrote the check and hurried out.

Like the dear friend he was, Timothy tailed her home. During the drive her depression returned. To the casual observer, Diana appeared to have noth-ing to complain about, but if anyone ever scratched the surface, reality painted a different picture.

For the past year, she had been the sole care-taker of her ailing grandmother. The emotional strain alone often sent Diana spiraling out of con-trol while the financial aspect had her straddling the line to bankruptcy.

Cancer ravished their life savings and it seemed there wasn't an end in sight. Through it all, Diana kept her personal problems private and battled everything the best way she could. She didn't want, need, or accept handouts or pity.

Which is why it didn't make sense for her to be attracted to someone as self-centered as Marcel Tay-lor. The man counted on others to solve not only his business problems but his personal ones as well.

Why should she search for a woman who didn't want to be found? Diana had no doubts that if she were married to a man as emotionally challenged as Donald Taylor, she would need a vacation too.

She moaned. Her usual spiel wasn't working. In the past, anger diffused her attraction to Taylor—but not lately.

A while later, she arrived at the Gables Apartments

and pulled into her reserved space. She checked her watch and figured out that she had less than an hour to get her grandmother to the oncologist.

Timothy parked next to her as she jumped out of her car. "Has anyone ever told you that you drive like a bat out of hell?"

"Just everyone I know," she yelled over her shoulder while she rushed toward her building. Seconds later, she breezed into her apartment.

Vicki, the part-time nurse, and her grandmother, Louisa Mae, looked up from the sofa when Diana entered the living room.

Her grandmother smiled and tugged the white scarf around her head. "Hey, sweetie. You're home early." She patted the vacant cushion on her right. "Come watch the stories with us."

Diana's hands settled on her hips. "Nana, how come you're not ready?"

"I'm not going," Louisa said, using the remote to turn up the television.

"What do you mean you're not going?"

Vicki stood and pushed back a lock of red hair as her green gaze met Diana's. "Time to make my grand exit."

Diana watched her gather her things from the coffee table.

"Good luck," Vicki whispered as she passed Diana.

Once she heard the front door close behind the nurse, Diana turned her attention to her grandmother. "Please, let's not fight over this today."

Louisa shrugged. "Who's fighting?"

"All right, then. Do you need me to help you get dressed?"

"No." She locked gazes with Diana. "I said I wasn't going."

Diana stared. What else could she do—throw a fit, hold her breath until she passed out?

Louisa smiled again. "Oh, stop looking at me like that. It isn't the end of the world." She punched the power button on the remote and the living room fell silent. After a few seconds, she said, "I'm tired of being sick."

"Then let's go to your appointment so you can get better."

She shook her head sadly. "Chemotherapy is killing me, not cancer. Going through that stuff is inhumane. I'd rather you just dragged me outside by my hair and shoot me a few times."

Diana drew in a sharp breath. "Nana—"

"I'm not going."

Her grandmother's hard tone left no room for argument and Diana reconsidered holding her breath. Defeated, she clunked over to the armchair next to the sofa and plopped down. "Fine. You don't want to go, then I'm not going to make you."

"Good."

"Why should I care if my last surviving relative wants to give up and die on me?"

Louisa shook her head as a light chuckle filled the room. "The guilt thing isn't going to work this time, sweetie. I fell for that last week."

Diana clamped her mouth closed and felt the sting of tears around her eyes.

Louisa inched closer to the chair and reached for Diana's hand.

"If you don't go, you'll die," Diana said.

"Suffering through that kind of therapy is no

way to live." Louisa squeezed her hand. "I want to enjoy the time I have left. Not only that, but I want to see you happy again. No more worrying about the future and medical bills we can't afford."

"Is that what this is about?" Diana leaned forward, convinced she had found the real reason behind Louisa's rash behavior.

"It's part of it, but by no means all of it." Louisa's gaze softened as she scanned Diana's face. "I worry so much about you."

"Me?"

"Yes, you. You've been through so much and at such a young age."

"I'm thirty, Nana."

"Still a child," she said gently. "I wish I could shoulder a fraction of the load you carry, then maybe the world wouldn't seem so heavy."

Against Diana's will a tear trickled down her face and she quickly wiped it away. "I'm going to be just fine. *We're* going to be fine."

Louisa continued as if she hadn't heard her. "Do you know, I can't remember the last time I heard you laugh. At your age you should be having the time of your life—dating different men every day of the week."

"Ha," Diana exclaimed at the absurdity. "Maybe you should get a CT scan next."

Louisa frowned. "I'm serious."

"I know. That's what makes this conversation scary." Diana eased out of her shoes. "Men are the last thing on my mind," she lied smoothly as she pushed all thoughts of Marcel out of her head.

"I'm not saying you have to marry and settle down before I kick the bucket. I'm not one of those who believe women can only be happy when they're barefoot and pregnant. But I do want to see you loosen up a bit. Let your hair down—even if it's just for a little while."

The sincerity in Louisa's eyes touched Diana but she felt awkward, even embarrassed, about discussing her lackluster love life.

"We're supposed to be talking about you."

"We are. We're discussing my wish to see you happy. I don't care if it's with a man, woman, dog, animal, vegetable, or mineral." She chuckled. "I need to leave this world knowing you have something that brings joy into your life. Is that too much to ask?"

Stumped, Diana tightened her grasp on Louisa's hand. "No," she said, wiping a few more tears from her eyes. "It's not too much to ask."

Five

Brandy's big, wet, sloppy kisses were always the highlight of Marcel's day. At ninety pounds, the Doberman pinscher had a ferocious bark and a low growl that frightened and intimidated strangers. Few people knew the dog's theatrics were all an act.

"How's my girl doing?" Marcel asked, scratching behind the dog's ear.

Brandy's jaw sagged as her eyes rolled back with pleasure.

"Daddy missed his little girl," he cooed as if talking to a real baby. Pushing up from bended knee, Marcel continued into the house. To his relief, the place was empty of maids, chefs, and the occasional freeloader.

Panting, Brandy trotted next to her master into the kitchen where she was promptly rewarded with a doggie treat.

"It doesn't take much to make you happy, does it?" he asked at her exuberance.

Brandy barked.

"I didn't think so." He tossed her another treat, and then went to the refrigerator to find something for himself. "I wish we could trade places for a day," he said. "I'd love to lounge around on Italian leather all day."

Brandy looked around as if to say, *Who, me?*

Marcel laughed. He would probably never break Brandy's habit of relaxing on his expensive furniture whenever he wasn't around.

Taking out all the items he needed for a good sub sandwich, Marcel broke the news of his parents' possible divorce to his "little girl." He took her silent attentiveness as concern. Most likely Brandy was simply waiting for him to drop or toss her a piece of whatever he was fixing.

"I mean, have you ever heard of anyone getting a divorce after forty years?"

Woof!

"My point exactly." Marcel piled more condiments onto his sandwich. "This puts everything we talked about the other night in a whole new light, don't you think? Finding a woman and settling down is supposed to be permanent. Now that I think about it, almost everyone I know is on either their second or third marriage.

"A lot of them have two or three different sets of children. Not to mention the children they have with people they never married. It's crazy." He glanced at Brandy.

She lay down and placed her head in between her front paws.

"This doesn't mean I'm reneging on finding you a mom. I'm just saying that maybe it's going to take a little more time and thought. If I'm going to do this, then I want to do it right and only one time."

Brandy moaned and continued to look pitiful.

"I promise. I'm not trying to back out of this." He sliced his sub in half and struggled to fit it on his plate. "Hell, I don't know what I'm saying." He turned and walked out of the kitchen. It took him a few seconds to realize that Brandy hadn't followed him.

"Stop being a drama queen and come on," he said over his shoulder, heading into the entertainment room. When she still refused to come, he rolled his eyes and settled into his favorite spot on the leather sofa and activated the plasma television by voice command.

In the back of his mind, he knew it was crazy to be annoyed by his dog's behavior, but he couldn't help it. He also couldn't help feeling defensive about the whole settling down issue.

One woman, for the rest of his life.

A shiver raced down his spine. Why did the idea sound so ludicrous to him now when this morning it had filled him with such longing?

"Maybe Solomon is right. I need to see a therapist."

Brandy finally trotted into the room as if sensing that her job as confidante was in jeopardy.

Marcel shook his head and crammed a corner of his sandwich into his mouth. He reviewed the situation with his parents again in his mind and became fairly confident that this was just a bleep in their relationship and that the whole thing could probably be resolved if his father just apologized for whatever he'd done. Even if he didn't know what he'd done, an apology went a long way with women.

He frowned at that thought. Diana was mad at

him. Had he forgotten to do something? Maybe it was her birthday. Nah, her birthday was December 15. Funny how he seemed to remember that.

Di. He smiled, liking the nickname. Actually, he'd always like the name Diana. It was beautiful and elegant. Not to take anything from his secretary, but it seemed that she went out of her way to be invisible.

Once, he'd taken the time to study her. Which wasn't unusual. He'd assessed most, no, all of the women working for him at one time or another. He'd found Diana to have the most beautiful skin he'd ever seen. And that was without the aid of makeup. Clean, clear, beautiful skin. Was that a commercial?

However, her most adorable feature was her nose. It was the tiniest bit off-centered. He doubted that the average person even noticed. Who knows, maybe she didn't know. He frequently wondered how she would look with her hair down. In the two years he'd known her, it was always pulled into a simple ponytail.

Sighing, he pulled himself out of his daydream and realized he needed to get ready to head down to the club. It was time to be Mr. Nightlife again.

He handed Brandy the last portion of his meal and pushed himself up from the sofa. "Time to get back to work. Who knows, maybe I'll meet the lady of our dreams tonight."

Woof!

An excited Tim clutched Diana's hand. "Why don't you and I go clubbing tonight?"

Diana groaned as she loaded the dishwasher. "Not

my scene. I put up with enough loud music and
lurid acts at work."

"I know. I'm jealous, too." He helped her out by
scrubbing and wiping down the counters. "But how
are you ever going to meet Mr. Right locked up in
this apartment all the time?"

"Don't you start on me, too. I've already had
this conversation once today."

"Yeah, well. If my two cents count for anything, I
agree with your grandma."

"Color me surprised." She closed the dishwasher
and turned it on. "The thing is, I'm not so sure that
a relationship is what I want right now."

"Of course you do." Tim frowned. "No one wants
to grow old alone. Anyone who tells you different
is lying to themselves."

Diana remained adamant. "I don't need a man
to complete me."

"More lies."

"Tim!"

"What?" He plopped the sponge down and faced
her. "I'm just being truthful. Or are you really one
of those women who buy into that 'I am woman;
hear me roar' crap?"

"It's not crap," she snapped with more force than
was warranted. "A woman's value is much more
than being submissive to a man's every whim."

He held up his hand like a brick wall. "Two is always better than one: two orgasms, two incomes,
or his and his matching Mercedes. Okay?"

Diana laughed.

"Besides, you're not fooling anyone, Miss Thang.
I know you have the hots for Casanova Brown. Isn't
that what you said your boss's friends call him?"

"Not hardly." Diana's laugh was stiff and unnatural. "He's the most self-centered, spoiled individual I've ever met. Hell, I think it's pathetic how most of the women at the office fawn over him."

"Personally, if I worked there I would never get anything done. What is the name of that cologne he wears? I must buy some for Caleb."

"Ralph Lauren Purple Label," she said. Looking at Tim's lopsided grin, she added, "I've had to purchase it for him before."

"Uh-huh." Tim crossed his arms and leaned back against the counter. "Let me ask you something," he said, giving her a long measuring stare. "Would you admit you have a crush on him?"

Diana hesitated and, as a result, gave Tim his answer.

"I didn't think so."

"Whatever," she mumbled under her breath. Shaking her head, she turned and headed out of the kitchen.

Dressed in pink pajamas, Louisa settled into her favorite spot on the sofa. She was the picture of a perfect, cute little old grandmother with a quilted blanket across her legs and a white silk scarf around her thinning hair.

Louisa glanced up from the television as Tim and Diana entered. "Are you two going out?"

Tim shook his head as he plopped down next to Louisa. "I've asked, but as usual she won't go."

"I'm not stopping you from going," Diana said. "Of course, Caleb might have something to say when he gets back into town."

"Is he paying you to keep an eye on me or something? That's the second time you threatened me today."

"No."

"Good."

"I offered to do it for free."

Tim rolled his eyes. "Figures."

"I think you should go." Louisa clapped her hands. "Go to one of those discos and have a good time."

"Discos?" Diana laughed, settling into an armchair. "Disco has been dead for a while, Nana."

"There's Bell Bottoms in midtown. It's a seventies club. That would be a great place to play dress-up." Tim grew excited. "I'm sure I have a pair of platform shoes somewhere in my closet."

"Why would anyone have platforms in their closet?"

He shrugged. "For emergencies."

"Then what do they call those dance halls nowadays?" Louisa asked.

"Clubs," Diana and Tim answered.

"So go to one of those."

"I can't, Nana. I have a lot of work to catch up on before dragging myself into the office tomorrow." She sighed, not really wanting to work either.

"There should be a law against working on Saturday," Tim complained. "Corporate America really stiffs you by making you a salaried employee versus paying you hourly."

"What are you complaining about? You're a housewife or househusband. Besides, it's not like I didn't know what I was getting into when I took the job. The music industry keeps moving seven days a week."

"Stop changing the subject," Louisa huffed. "Diana, I really think you should go out to one of these club thingies. You know, I met your grandfather at a dance hall."

"You met him at a strip club," Diana corrected.

"Actually, it was more burlesque. We left a little more to the imagination." A dreamy gleam sparkled in her eyes. "Ah, I knew quite a few moves back in my day."

Tim clutched Louisa's hand. "You are my idol."

Louisa blushed and shooed him away.

Diana rolled her eyes. "Both of you worry me."

"Don't waste your time worrying about me." Louisa's attention returned to her granddaughter. "I've had my fun. It's your turn."

"Well, maybe another time." Diana stood. "I have other things to do."

There was no mistaking her grandmother's disappointed stare, but at Louisa's next words, Diana stopped in her tracks.

"Tim, I think I'd like to go with you to one of those clubs tonight."

"Do what?" Diana blinked.

"You would?" Tim clapped his hands in delight. "That would be great."

"No, it won't." Diana's hard stare shifted to him. "Don't encourage her."

"I think it'll be fun." Louisa pushed herself up from the sofa. "I wonder what I should wear."

"Nana, you're not going to a club."

Louisa's chin tilted up in defiance. "I don't see why not. I'm over twenty-one."

Diana's hands settled on her hips. "I'm not worried about you being carded. I'm worried about your health."

"I'm fine." Louisa waved off her concern and looked back at Tim. "Let's go see what's in my closet."

He jumped to his feet. "Goody."

"Wait," Diana interjected, not liking the way her grandmother brushed her off. "I can't allow you to go."

Now Louisa's hand settled on her hips. "I don't remember asking for your permission. I'll do what I want to do. And I want to go to the disco ... I mean, the club with Tim. If you're so concerned about my health, then you can come and watch over me."

Diana's eyes narrowed. "Why, you scheming little old lady."

Louisa grinned. "You don't have to go. No one's twisting your arm." She looked over at Tim. "Let's go look for something in my closet."

Smirking, Tim offered Louisa his arm and together they left a steaming Diana in the center of the living room.

"You really are my idol," Tim whispered.

"Yeah." Louisa chuckled. "Sometimes I amaze myself."

Six

Club Secrets had a reputation for being one of the hottest spots in Atlanta and, judging by the long line behind the velvet rope, the hardest place to get into.

"I don't know about this," Diana said, stepping out of Tim's car. Her eyes zeroed in on what the women in line were wearing and immediately she felt over-dressed.

"Oh. This is going to be exciting," Louisa said. Her eyes were the size of silver dollars. At seventy-two, she wore a black and gold pantsuit, gold looped earrings, and her favorite Beverly Johnson wig.

Diana, too, wore a pantsuit, but it was a black and white number that was more suited for a business meeting than a social function. Her hair remained pulled back in its tried and true ponytail while her makeup consisted of only a single coat of ruby-red lipstick.

Tim, however, looked as though he'd stepped out of the pages of *GQ*. His enthusiasm for going out for the evening matched Louisa's.

Everyone closed their doors and the car alarm was engaged before Tim walked around from the driver's side. "Are you ladies ready for a good time?" he asked, offering each of them his arm.

"Oh, my." Louisa pointed. "Look at that one woman over there. She's naked."

"Nana, don't point," Diana whispered. "It's rude."

"And that one over there. On second thought, is she even old enough to get into this place?"

"Probably not." Tim chuckled and led them to the back of the line. "It's none of our business one way or another."

"Humph," Louisa said under her breath and then looked around the crowd to find more fashion victims. "Oh, look, Diana. That young man looks like a nice handsome boy. Maybe you should go and say hi to him."

A few people snickered around them, including Tim.

Diana closed her eyes and shrank two inches from total mortification.

"Oh, what about that nice young man over there?"

"Nana," Diana hissed. "Will you stop? You're embarrassing me."

"I'm doing no such thing." Louisa frowned. "I'm just trying to help."

Tim laughed. "I can tell already this is going to be one hell of an evening."

"I'll agree on the hell part." Diana sulked.

* * *

Champagne and gorgeous women overflowed the VIP room of Club Secrets when Marcel and Solomon entered. Navigating through the room, Marcel smiled and shook hands with nearly everyone present. Most pressed him about checking out one group or another, some even handed him demo tapes.

It was hard to get used to everyone always wanting something from him. Most days, he managed just fine. Others were a struggle—like tonight.

"Tee Bo, my man." He stretched his hands and greeted the ex–pro football player turned club owner. "The party is off the chain as usual."

"Of course, Casanova. Tee Bo always knows how to throw a party." He slid his arm around Marcel's shoulder and gestured to the array of women he'd chosen to entertain VIP guests for the evening. *"Mi casa es su casa."* If you see anything you like, you better hang on to it."

Solomon glided up next to them. "Sometimes I feel like a kid in a candy store."

Marcel grinned. "Too bad you're a diabetic."

"This is true." He held up his glass of champagne and the two lifelong friends clinked their glasses together.

Being a fan of old-school rap, Marcel found his attention quickly drawn to the deejay scratching on the ones and twos. He moved to the balcony of the VIP room and stared down at the crowd below. "Hey, is that the cat you were telling me about from the radio station?"

Tee Bo and Solomon moved next to him.

"Yeah, bananas, ain't he?" Tee Bo said.

"No doubt. I need to book him to do my next birthday bash."

"For you, I'm sure he'd consider it an honor."

Marcel scanned the crowd, and for a second a familiar face caught his attention and then vanished. Frowning, he looked through the crowd again and was disappointed when he couldn't find what he was looking for.

"Is something wrong?" Solomon asked.

Giving up his search, Marcel shook his head. "No. I just thought I saw someone, that's all. It's crazy, really. No way would she come to a place like this."

"Who?"

"Di—no one. Forget it."

Diana, Tim, and Louisa finally found an empty table midway between the dance floor and the rest room. In no time, a waitress magically appeared at their table to ask for their drink order.

Louisa and Tim both ordered a gin and tonic while Diana declared herself the designated driver and ordered a soda.

"Isn't this marvelous?" Louisa shouted, leaning over toward Diana. "There are so many beautiful people here."

Diana rolled her eyes, still not believing that she was coerced into coming.

Tim reached across the table and placed his hand on hers. "You're here now. You might as well just loosen up and try to relax."

Her eyes narrowed on Tim while the music's bass boomed in perfect harmony with her growing headache. Who could possibly relax with a decibel level threatening to puncture her eardrum?

"I'm going to get you both back for this," she shouted. "Mark my words."

A nice tall brother, sporting Sean John attire, stopped and stood in between Diana and her grandmother.

"Hello, ladies. How are you doing this evening?"

Diana stiffened and refused to meet the stranger's eyes.

"We're doing great," Louisa cooed, propping an elbow up on the table and cradling her chin in her hand. "Do you come here often?" she asked.

Diana couldn't believe her ears. Was her grandmother actually going to pick the guy up next?

"I've been here a few times," the stranger replied, amusement lacing in his voice. "What about you?"

Diana glanced up at the guy and was impressed by the man's well-groomed features. When his striking hazel eyes slid in her direction, she quickly glanced away again.

"It's my first time here," Louisa shouted and smiled as if the man were Harry Belafonte. "Both mine and Diana's first time." She touched her granddaughter's hand. "Isn't that right, sweetheart?"

Diana's skin crawled with humiliation. "Right, *Granny.*"

The old woman just chuckled and batted her eyes playfully up at him. Diana started believing that there might be something to the movie *Invasion of the Body Snatchers,* because she truly didn't know or understand the woman pretending to be Louisa tonight.

"By the way, I'm Louisa. My good friends call me Lou." She batted her faux eyelashes again. "As you know, this is my grandbaby, Diana. Diana, please say hi to the man."

Sighing, Diana forced her gaze upward. "Hi." For her lackluster performance, she immediately received a swift kick from under the table. "Ouch!"

"Hello. I'm Alan." He glanced between the women, then over at the only person yet to be introduced.

"Oh, where are our manners?" Louisa continued to holler over the music. "This is our good friend and neighbor, Timothy Banks."

"Hello, Tim."

"Hello."

The men's hands reached across the table for a brief handshake.

"Well, I actually came over for a dance partner," Alan said.

"Oh, she would love to." Louisa clapped her hands.

"Nana!"

Louisa's sunny smile beamed over at her granddaughter. "What?"

Alan cleared his throat. "Actually . . . I was asking Tim."

Louisa's smile flat-lined as she slowly turned her attention to her neighbor.

Tim, however, perked up. "I'd love to." He jumped up from his chair and tossed a wink over at Diana.

After Tim and Alan left the table it took all the restraint Diana had not to burst out laughing.

Louisa looked at her granddaughter. "What just happened here?"

"Nothing that you didn't deserve." Diana smirked.

Their drinks arrived at the table and Diana grumbled about having to pay for them.

"Are you going to act like this the whole night?" Louisa asked, frowning. "No wonder you have trouble meeting men. Don't you ever smile?"

"Not if I can help it." Diana flashed her teeth, but the grimace didn't remotely resemble a smile.

Louisa shook her head. "You get that contrary spirit from your father's side of the family. He didn't care for smiling too much either."

The barb stung, mainly because she didn't know much about her father and she didn't want to associate anything negative with what little she did know. In the next moment, some young buck appeared at the table and this time asked Louisa to the dance floor.

"Nana, I really don't—"

"Oh, relax. I didn't come here tonight just to watch you sulk in the corner." Louisa stood from the chair and clutched on to the twenty-something man's arm. "I'll be fine."

There wasn't a point to arguing, Diana soon learned, as Louisa laughed her way to the dance floor.

Diana's pride suffered a massive blow when she realized that a seventy-two-year-old woman was picked over her. "I'm more hopeless than I thought." She rolled her eyes heavenward and prayed for strength to get through the evening.

A man on the balcony of the second floor caught her attention. "Mr. Taylor," she whispered.

Her gaze remained glued on him while he laughed and hobnobbed with model-thin women in expensive stilettos. Jealousy hit her like a brick wall as she watched them press against him for photo ops or to slip him their numbers. "It must be nice to have the whole world on a silver platter," she mumbled.

She forced her gaze away just as another man approached her table.

"Care to dance?"

"No, thanks."

He held up his hands in surrender. "Sorry. I didn't mean any harm. It's just when I see a beautiful woman sitting all alone, I figure I can at least attempt to cheer her up by asking her to dance."

"I don't dance," she said, shifting her attention to the dance floor to see if she could spot her grandmother.

"You don't dance?" The man laughed and then eased into the chair next to her. "Then what are you doing at a club?"

"Minding my own business and trying to set an example for others."

"Ooh, that's a good one." He held out his hand. "My name is Bennie. What's yours?"

Diana finally looked at him and was shocked to see the man with shiny finger waves and his two front teeth capped in gold. She cleared her throat. "Look, Bennie. I don't mean to be rude but I'm really not interested."

"Surely you're not going to shoot a brother down like that. At least allow me to buy you a drink."

Her patience held on by a thin thread. "Look, I came with someone."

"You mean the old lady and the gay guy?"

She frowned.

Bennie's smile slid wider. "I've been watching you all night. You don't have a man."

"Actually," a smooth familiar voice cut in, "she's with me."

Diana glanced up at the man behind Bennie and she blinked in surprise at seeing Marcel Taylor smiling down at them.

Seven

The world melted away as Diana stared up at her boss. Once she realized what she was doing, embarrassment burned her cheeks and she glanced away.

"Mr. Taylor." Bennie jutted out his hand. "My main man. Whatcha doing here? Man, I love your work."

"Is that right?" Marcel smiled, but ignored the offered hand. "I'm always glad to meet a fan." He swung his sparkling gaze in Diana's direction. "Good evening, Diana."

"Hello."

"So, you really know this chick?" Bennie asked in awe.

Marcel nodded and maintained his brilliant smile. "We've been together for the past two years."

Bennie's beady gaze returned and raked over her. She could hear the man wondering why Marcel Taylor would be interested in such a plain "chick."

"All right, then," he said, backing away. "I didn't mean no disrespect."

"I appreciate that," Marcel said.

Bennie grabbed a napkin off the table and then reached inside his eggplant-colored suit for a tape. "Uh. Do you think that maybe I could get you to listen to this tape? My cousin's wife's nephew does a little rappin'."

"You probably should try to get that to one of our scouts," Marcel said kindly.

Diana sighed and shook her head. A few seconds later, the man stumbled out another apology before he finally left the table.

"I thought that he would never leave," Diana said.

Marcel laughed. "Mind if I join you?" he asked, gesturing to the vacant chair next to her.

She'd rather he didn't, but shrugged instead. "It's a free country."

He frowned at her answer as he sat down. "You're still mad at me about something."

Before she had the chance to answer, two scantily clad women rushed up to Marcel. Her ever-accommodating boss was only too happy about the attention. He answered their questions about auditioning for his label and then turned his attention back to Diana.

"So what did I do?" Marcel asked once they were alone again.

Diana sipped her drink. "I told you earlier that I'm not mad. I just have a lot on my mind."

"And Michael Jackson really is Peter Pan," he joked and finally wrangled a smile out of her. "Ah, now we're getting somewhere. Come on, I can't fix something unless I know it's broken."

There was no way Diana was going to tell him

the truth: that she didn't like finding him and Nora huddled together in the elevator. Admitting something like that would be the kiss of death.

Marcel reached over and turned her chin in his direction so she would meet his gaze. "You're important to me. If I did something, please tell me."

Sweet words, she thought, even though he meant them professionally.

"Oh, Diana," Louisa shouted, returning to the table. Who's your friend?" She laid her hand against Marcel's shoulder and smiled brightly at him. "My, you're handsome. I bet you've been told that before."

Diana rolled her eyes. "He's not my friend, Nana," Diana said. "He's my boss."

"Ouch." Marcel straightened in his chair. "That hurt." He draped an arm around her. "I'd like to think that we're friends as well."

Awareness jolted through her body, but she pretended not to notice. "Grandma, this is Marcel Taylor. Mr. Taylor, my grandmother, Louisa Styles."

"Friends call me Lou," she said, batting her lashes again and offering him her hand.

"Lou Styles." Marcel rolled the name around a few times as he removed his arm from Diana's shoulder to shake Louisa's hand. "Catchy. Ever considered showbiz?"

"Actually, I used to be a dancer."

"Really? Professionally?"

"Yes, I—"

"So how long have you been here?" Diana jumped in before her grandmother regaled them with tales of her glory days as a stripper.

"A couple of hours. You brought your grandmother out to a club?"

"Brought—no. Supervise—yes."

He laughed. "That's certainly different."

"I'd like to see how you handle a mentally insane senior citizen," she deadpanned.

Marcel's body continued to tremble. "You're funny, Di. I like that."

"Ahem." Louisa cleared her throat. "Just in case you forgot, I'm still standing here."

Diana caught the casual use of her nickname and the way his tone softened as he said it. Then again, she could've just imagined it. Probably did.

"Why don't you and your grandmother join me in the VIP room?" His smile beamed at Louisa. "I'm sure I can get everyone to be on their best behavior."

"That's all right," Diana answered before Louisa raved about how wonderful or how much fun it would be. "We're fine down here."

Marcel's dark gaze shifted back to her and entrapped hers. "There's that cold chill again."

"You're imagining things," she said, forcing her eyes away. "I'm not angry with you." Though she wasn't looking at him, she could feel his stare.

"Do I have your word on that?"

His hand brushed against hers and a delicious warmth rippled through her. "You have my word," she said, once again lifting her eyes.

"Yo, Casanova." A large hand pounded on Marcel's back. "Spread the love." Tee Bo laughed before looking at Diana. "Ms. Guy, what are you doing here?"

Working for Marcel, Diana knew just about everyone in the entertainment business and that included nightclub owners.

"Hey, Tee Bo. I'm just hanging out . . . with my grandmother." She gestured to Louisa.

"Oh, snap. You brought your granny in here?"

"My goodness, you're tall," Louisa said, tilting back. "You must have giantism in your family or something."

"Nana," Diana hissed.

"What?"

Tee Bo's massive arm dropped around Louisa's shoulders and Diana feared her grandmother's knees would buckle. "To tell you the truth, Granny, I'm the only one in my family this size. My father was the tallest at five eleven until I came along. Ain't that something?"

"Excuse me, Mr. Taylor." A honey-coated, feminine voice interrupted them.

Marcel turned toward a Caribbean goddess with large doe-shaped eyes and a Colgate smile. The men's eyes bulged and then slowly traveled down the woman's curvy frame.

Diana watched fascinated at how the woman playfully batted her eyes and leaned in close to give a better view of her cleavage. Did she and Diana's grandmother go to the same school of flirtation?

"I was wondering if I could pass you this demo tape."

"Are you a singer?" Marcel asked, accepting the tape.

"Well, I'm actually a singer-slash-rapper-slash-dancer—"

Slash-ho. Diana glanced away and wished that she were anywhere but here.

Before long, a crowd gathered, each person vying for Marcel's undivided attention. Even Tim and Alan returned and stood around her boss like starry-eyed puppies. What made things so bad for Diana was the realization that she was no different than any of them. Marcel, too, fascinated her. She was just determined not to show it.

"Waitress," Diana called, lifting her glass. "Can I get a refill?" She refrained from asking for a splash of alcohol. When she returned her attention to her boss, she caught the punch line of a joke before everyone erupted into laughter.

Louisa ducked out of sight and tugged Tim along with her.

"Is something wrong, Lou?" he asked.

"No, no. I'm fine. I have a plan," she whispered. "Do you know whether this Mr. Taylor drove here himself?"

"What?" He had trouble hearing over the loud music.

Grabbing a corner of his shirt, she tugged him down to her level. "I have a plan. Now, pay attention. . . ."

Diana watched how Marcel handled the growing crowd of women with ease. She was even beginning to admire the way he'd mastered the art of flirting without being obvious. Casanova Brown, indeed.

"Diana," Louisa said, inching her way over to her. "Do you mind if we go home now?"

"What's wrong? Are you not feeling well?"

"I'm fine," she said, pressing a trembling hand

up to her temple. "I'm just very tired all of a sudden."

"Of course, sure." Diana jumped up from the table and glanced around. "Tim?" she called several times, scanning the people around them. "Where did he go?"

"Diana?" Louisa said.

"Just a sec, Nana." Diana grasped her hand. "We have to find Tim." She forced calm into her voice. "He was just here a moment ago."

"Is there a problem, Di?" Marcel asked.

"You didn't happen to see where Tim went?"

He, too, looked around. "I could've sworn—"

"Diana, I need to lie down."

Marcel frowned. "Is she all right? She doesn't look too good."

"No, she's not. I have to get her home but it looks like our ride has disappeared."

"Your boyfriend left you?"

"He's not my boyfriend," she said, impatiently. "And if I ever get my hands on him, I'll kill him."

"I can take you home," Marcel offered and then glanced at his watch. "I've put in enough time."

"No, that won't be necessary."

"Diana," Louisa moaned.

"I don't mind," Marcel pressed as he leveled his concerned gaze on Louisa.

"But Tim—"

"He can see his own way home. I want to make sure nothing happens to your Nana."

Tee Bo tuned into the conversation. "Is something wrong with Granny?"

"She's not feeling too well," Marcel informed him. "We're going to head out." They slapped hands in a friendly handshake and gave each other a one-shoulder hug. "I'll catch ya later."

"No doubt," Tee Bo said and then leaned down to plant a kiss on Louisa's pudgy cheek. "You take care of yourself, Granny. I want to see you back in here soon."

Louisa's face blushed burgundy. "You can count on that."

"Well, I wouldn't," Diana said sternly before looking back at her boss.

"The offer is still good," he said.

She cast another futile glance around and relented at her grandmother's obvious exhaustion. "Okay. If it's not too much trouble."

His full lips captured her attention when they eased into a wide smile. "It's no trouble at all."

Eight

First Marcel welcomed any excuse to leave Club Secrets. His heart just wasn't into smiling and posing for the cameras, though he'd put on a good show. Making appearances at the hottest clubs was just another part of his job.

Stepping out of the loud club and into the night's cool air was an instant relief. Despite the hour drawing near one A.M., a crowd remained outside trying to get into the packed club.

"You really are popular," Louisa commented. "It's like you're a movie star or something."

"Not quite," he said, waving to the crowd. "But you'd be amazed at how many people in this town are trying to break into the music business."

"It's awfully nice of you to take us home," Lou said, smiling.

He grinned. "Don't be silly. It's my pleasure." His gaze slid to Diana and it seemed that she made a conscious effort to avoid his stare.

When a stretch limousine pulled up in front of them, Lou gasped. "Is this yours?"

Marcel nodded and enjoyed the look of excitement plastered on the older woman's face. "My job comes with a few perks."

Lou clapped her hands. "I'd say. Diana, isn't it gorgeous?"

"Yes, Nana. It's very nice."

There was that tone again, Marcel noted. What the hell had he done? Maybe he should take a page of his own advice and apologize for any and all things.

Charlie Lopez, Marcel's driver for the past eight years, jumped out of the limo and rushed around to open their door.

"Ah, Ms. Guy," Charlie said when his gaze landed on Diana. "A pleasure to see you this evening."

"Good evening, Charlie. I see you're back from vacation. How was it?"

"Great. We'll have to get together again so I can tell you about it."

"Sounds like a date."

She smiled and Marcel was painfully aware that her attitude toward Charlie was a hell of a lot friendlier. And what did she mean by *date?*

"We're taking Diana and her grandmother home," Marcel said.

"Grand . . . Louisa?" His eyes widened as he recognized the woman standing beside Marcel. "Well, I'll be damned. Tonight is just full of surprises."

"You can't keep a wild tiger caged for long," Louisa singsonged.

The men laughed and helped her into the limo.

"Don't worry, Charlie," Diana said, patting him on the arm. "I'll tell you the whole story later."

Charlie smiled. "I look forward to hearing the details."

When they laughed, Marcel felt excluded from their obvious friendship. It was odd to be bothered by that, he realized, but he was.

Once inside, Marcel continued to be amused by Lou's fascination with her surroundings. However, Diana looked bored. Limousines were nothing new to his secretary. In fact, seeing them was nearly an everyday event. Still, he wondered what it would take to impress her. Was she the kind of woman who lit up for diamonds and pearls or was she the kind who was blown away by the little things?

Charlie pulled out into traffic and Marcel reached for the intercom button. "What's the address?"

"Charlie knows where it is," Louisa said before Diana had the opportunity to speak. "He's been to the apartment several times."

"Oh?" Marcel's gaze sought Diana's. "I never knew you two were such good buddies."

"There's a lot you don't know about me," she said softly and then returned her attention to the view outside her window.

Her words socked him in the gut and the unexpected blow startled him, probably because there was a ring of truth to them. Hadn't their conversation this afternoon proved that fact?

"There's champagne in here," Lou marveled, finding the icebox.

"Don Perignon Brut Rose Champagne; the best," he boasted proudly. "Would you like some?"

"I'd love—"

"No." Diana's stern look silenced any protest her grandmother contemplated.

"Sorry," Marcel felt obligated to say. "I didn't mean to . . . uh, get anyone in trouble."

Lou dropped back against the seat and crossed her arms. "No need to apologize. It's not your fault my grandbaby is a fuddy-duddy."

Diana's jaw slacked and then tightened. "I'm only trying to look after you since you don't seem to be up for the job anymore."

Lou simply waved off the comment.

There was nothing like being caught in the middle of a family feud, Marcel thought. And this one had the markings of bitterness.

As he glanced between the two silent women, questions filled his head about exactly what was going on. Unfortunately, he didn't have the right to ask or expect an answer.

Silence encircled the small group and made the long ride feel more like the final walk down death row. As he turned to stare out his own window, he caught sight of a single tear escaping from Diana's glossy eyes.

"What's wrong, Diana?"

She shook her head and wiped her face dry. "Nothing."

Marcel blinked at the obvious lie. Why wouldn't she tell him what was bothering her? Why wouldn't she consider him a friend as well as her boss?

He glanced out his window, glad that her reflection showed in the tinted glass where he was free to watch her without being obvious.

Lou leaned forward and reached for her granddaughter's hand.

Diana seized the hand and gave it a reassuring pat. "Are you feeling better?"

"A little. I'll be fine once I crawl into bed."

Diana nodded and looked somewhat relieved. "Maybe we should have left a note on Tim's car, telling him we've gone home or something. I don't think we should have just left him there like that."

"Oh, he'll be fine. Trust me."

Diana gave her a long, dubious stare. "You seem awfully sure about that."

Louisa settled back into her chair. "He's a grown man. He's more than capable of taking care of himself."

Diana's eyes narrowed, but she didn't say anything more.

Marcel liked the way Diana's eyes sparked with suspicion and even the rush of color to her cheeks whenever she was angry or embarrassed. Though he'd only seen those emotions a few times in their short history together, each one was memorable.

He watched as she now returned her gaze to the passing scenery outside her window. He even experienced an incredible urge to reach over and pull the elastic band from her hair and watch it tumble loose.

In Marcel's large dictionary of women, he decided that Diana Guy's picture belonged next to the word *cute*. She didn't overpower you by having too much of one thing. No gigantic silicone twins like Nora Gibson in A&R, nor did she have too much junk in her trunk like Erin Hall in accounting.

Everything on Diana came in a nice *cute* package. Frowning, he wondered why a man hadn't grabbed her up by now. Especially since he could easily see her surrounded by children.

The limo turned and Marcel read a whitewashed sign for the Gables Apartments. Knowing Diana's salary, Marcel was more than surprised at the fact that she didn't actually own a home.

"Well, here we are," Lou said, sighing.

Diana quickly gathered their things. "Thanks again for the ride, Mr. Taylor. I really appreciate it."

He stiffened. "You know, you can call me Marcel every once in a while."

She smiled and then glanced up at Charlie when the door opened.

Lou gave him a sympathetic pat on the arm and whispered, "She's just a little stressed tonight. It's not you."

Relieved, he nodded and followed them out of the limo. "Well, it was certainly nice to meet you, Lou. I hope our paths cross again soon." He leaned down and kissed the back of her hand.

"Be careful what you ask for," she said with a teasing lilt.

"If you're finished flirting, Nana, let's get you inside and into bed."

Then, like a silver-screen goddess, Louisa swooned.

"Nana!"

Marcel's keen reflexes kicked into gear and he caught her before she hit the ground. "I got her."

Charlie rushed to give him a helping hand.

Fear plastered Diana's features. "Maybe we should take her to the hospital."

"No, no," Lou moaned and clutched Marcel's arm. "Just help me inside."

"Of course," he said, sweeping her small frame into his arms. He knew Louisa was a small woman, but he marveled over just how little she weighed.

"Sir, I can do that for you," Charlie said.

"No, that's not necessary," Marcel and Lou said in unison.

Marcel frowned and wondered briefly if *Granny* was pulling their legs.

"I'm not so sure," Diana said. "Maybe you should have gone to your appointment today."

"Drop it, Diana." Lou rolled her eyes. "Now, if you could just kindly show this young man to our apartment, the sooner I can curl up in my warm bed."

Louisa might have appeared weak, but there was nothing fragile about her behavior. Marcel was convinced more than ever that the old lady was trying to pull the wool over his and Diana's eyes. But why?

"All right. Come on." Diana turned around and led the way to their apartment.

Once they were inside, Marcel's gaze soaked up every detail of the small apartment. The first thing he noticed was that they owned more furniture than the space allowed.

"Nice place you have here," he said, glancing around.

"It's home," Diana said. "Do you think you could carry her to her room?"

"Sure."

"We've only been in this apartment four months," Lou informed him. "For a while, we didn't think Diana would get the asking price of her house, but things came together and worked themselves out in the end."

"Nana, Mr. Taylor isn't interested in all of that." Diana opened a bedroom door.

Mr. Taylor again. "Actually, I find it quite interesting."

She said nothing, but gestured him into the room.

Marcel entered a pretty cream and gold room and placed Louisa on the bed. "Is there anything else I can do for you?"

"Chile, if I was just a few years younger, I—"

"Nana!"

Louisa rolled her eyes. "Fuddy-duddy."

Marcel smiled. "If I was a few years older, I might have taken you up on whatever you had in mind."

Louisa squealed and slapped him on the arm. "I like you."

"The feeling is mutual." He winked and then followed Diana.

"Nana, I'll be back to help you get ready for bed."

Louisa waved her off. "Don't bother. I can do it myself. I'm already feeling a lot better."

"But—"

"I can do it." Louisa sat up. "Now, git!"

Diana shook her head as she closed the door. "She's going to drive me crazy," she mumbled under her breath as she waltzed past Marcel.

Marcel chuckled. "It's probably because you two are opposites."

"No kidding."

When they made it to the foyer, Marcel stalled for time by asking, "So what's wrong with her?"

Diana's hand froze on the doorknob before she turned to face him. "What makes you think that there's something wrong with her?"

He shifted uncomfortably beneath her direct stare. "You said something about her missing an appointment."

She visibly relaxed. "Oh. Well, it's nothing."

Another lie. Marcel crossed his arms and gave her his own hard glare. "You know, I'm trying really hard not to be offended by your attitude toward me all night. And I have to tell you I'm not sure it's working."

Diana opened her mouth to respond, but then quickly closed it. "You're right. I'm being rude. Sorry."

He drew a deep breath and nodded. "It's okay. But it's clear to me that something's wrong. Let's talk about it. Maybe I can help."

Diana crossed her arms but she kept her tone civil. "I appreciate it, but you can't help. No one can." With that, she turned back toward the door and opened it. "Good night."

Marcel sighed and gave up. He certainly wasn't going to force her to talk to him. "All right. If that's the way you feel. Good night."

Diana's heart sank to the pit of her stomach as she watched Marcel stroll out of the apartment. Her enormous pride refused to let her stop him and, God forbid, ask for help.

Once he was gone, she closed the door and rested her head against it. Only then did she allow her tears to fall.

Nine

At five-thirty Saturday morning, a puffy-eyed Diana dragged out of bed, pulled on her jogging suit, and grabbed her MP3 player. Neither rain nor snow prevented Diana from starting her day with a four-mile run. It was what centered and rejuvenated her, which was exactly what she needed these days.

Stepping out of the apartment, she was surprised to see Tim was already out and waiting for her.

"I want details. Don't leave anything out," he said with a wide, knowing grin.

"What are you talking about?" She started her stretches. "Where did you disappear to last night?"

Tim's lips dipped dramatically. "Nothing happened last night?"

She stopped in the middle of a leg stretch to narrow her stare. "Were you expecting something to happen?"

"Well, Lou said—" He caught himself.

Understanding dawned on Diana. "I don't believe this." Last night's events scrolled through her head—mainly, Tim's sudden disappearance and Lou's lack of concern.

Tim held up his hands. "Now before you get upset."

"Why should I be upset? Louisa's meddling is a constant state in my life. She always knows what's best for everybody but her."

He relaxed.

"But you, on the other hand, should've known better. You're supposed to be my friend."

"I *am* your friend."

Her expression soured. "Some friend."

"Look, I saw the way you looked at Marcel. More importantly, I saw how he looked at you."

"What?" She shook her head. "Never mind. I don't want to know. The man is my boss. That's the beginning and the end of our relationship."

"The beginning, yes. The end, I'm not too sure." His gaze caught hers. "Just admit it. You like the guy."

Diana's irritation flared. "Listen to me: *I don't like Marcel Taylor.* Now get off my back." She jammed her headset on and blasted music into her ear before she took off running.

Marcel and Solomon linked up at Gold's Gym for their morning workout. Their dedication to physical fitness dated back to their adolescent years. But their dreams of being professional athletes died after a series of injuries in college. Nowadays, despite constant travel and conflicting schedules, the old friends still made time to make it to their favorite gym.

This morning, however, Marcel's mind strayed

during his treadmill run to travel back to the troubled eyes of Diana Guy. At the office, she was the ultimate business professional. She came to work on time, did her job, and never uttered a complaint. In essence, she was perfect for him—as a secretary, of course.

"So what do you know about Diana Guy?" Marcel asked suddenly, interrupting Solomon's recap of what had happened later that night at Club Secrets.

"Diana? Your secretary?"

"Yeah. I mean, have you ever heard anything about her—around the office or break room?"

Solomon lifted his water bottle from his treadmill's cup holder. "Gossip? You're asking me for gossip?"

"No, no. Not gossip, but, uh . . . information. She's so quiet and all."

"Yeah," I guess you're right," he said after thinking it over. "Come to think about it, I don't think I've seen her hanging out with any of the other employees. I've never heard a bad word spoken about her either."

Neither had Marcel. For someone he viewed as irreplaceable, she blended into the scenery so well it was amazing.

"Why are you so interested, anyway?"

Marcel shrugged and then accelerated the speed on his treadmill. "No reason. I was just curious."

Solomon's gaze remained glued to Marcel. "Since when are you 'just curious' when it comes to women? Come on, spill it."

"There's nothing to say. I just realized that I didn't know that much about her."

"And that's all?"

"Of course. What else would it be?"

* * *

Halfway through their run, Tim tapped Diana on the shoulder. When she ignored him, he reached out and moved the headset from her ear. "I'm sorry."

Diana slowed down.

"Oh, thank God," he moaned, grateful for a break from the crazy pace she'd set. "I thought you were going to kill me."

"I should," she huffed. "Maybe then I can get you and my grandmother to butt out of my personal life."

"Fine. I'll keep my nose out of your business."

"Promise?"

"Cross my heart and hope to die, stick a needle in my eye."

"Spare me the theatrics." She rolled her eyes, but allowed a grin to curve her lips. "It's kind of funny when I think about it."

"What Lou and I did?"

"No. That you two actually thought that Marcel and I would make a good couple." She laughed.

"What's so funny about that?"

"Only the obvious," she said, slowing down their run to a light jog. "We're complete opposites."

Tim laughed. "Unless he's gay, which I didn't detect on my radar, then I don't see a problem."

"Please. Marcel is this larger-than-life force that attracts everyone's attention. Every woman that comes within ten feet of him falls head over heels for the man. And me, I'm just . . . me."

"Still. He's just a man standing in front of a woman—"

"You need to stop watching so many Julia Roberts films."

"And you need to stop thinking that you're not worthy of someone like Marcel Taylor."

"It's not a question of worth. It's . . . I don't know." She came to a dead stop and glanced up at the dawn's growing sunrise.

Tim stopped as well. "What is it?"

Though Diana considered Tim to be her best friend, she didn't often divulge intimate details about herself. She kept pity parties to a minimum by keeping a lot to herself. Right now, she was in danger of breaking her own rule. "It's been my experience that hoping for things is usually a waste of time."

Tim frowned as he held her gaze. "That's not true."

"Of course it is." She started walking. "Like the time I hoped my biological father would show up one day with a perfectly good excuse for why he'd skipped out on me and my mom when I was nine months old." A tear strayed from her eye. "Or when I hoped the doctors caught my mother's breast cancer in time to save her."

"So now you don't hope to find love, is that it?"

She wiped her eyes and gave him a sad smile. "It's just a waste of time."

Diana breathed a little easier for the next two weeks. Marcel was on location for a video shoot for one of the label's newest artists. In the meantime, she took at least two calls an hour from Donald Taylor, who was on a misson to find his son. However, Marcel's single instruction during his absence was not to give his father his new cell phone number.

It wasn't an easy task.

"I guess he's taking his mother's side in all of this," Donald huffed.

Diana held her breath, unsure of what to say.

"All right, tell him I called *again*." He slammed the phone down.

"Yes, sir," she mumbled to a dial tone and hung up, too. Almost immediately, the phone rang again, but this time it was Marcel's missing-in-action mother, Camille.

"Mrs. Taylor, I'm so happy you called." Diana reached for her notepad. In the background, she heard music playing. "Where are you?"

"Enjoying a much needed vacation." She laughed. "My dear, if you've never been to Venice, you don't know what you're missing."

Diana smiled. She'd always liked Camille. "Some say ignorance is bliss."

"You have a point there. But life is to be enjoyed, my dear. You'll do good to remember that."

"I'll try."

"Good. Is my handsome son there? I think he might have hired some strange man to follow me around. At least, I hope. If not, I'll need to go to the local authorities."

"Oh, that would be Lee Castleman. I hired him . . . well, under Marcel's instructions. He was worried about you."

There was a long pause before Camille said, "I should've called him, I suppose." She sighed. "I just needed to get away. Have you ever felt like that?"

Diana rolled her eyes and nodded. "You have no idea."

"Then you should come out and join me." Camille perked up. "I could send you a ticket."

"I don't think so." Diana laughed, easing back into her chair. "My plate is sort of full right now."

Diana could tell that her answer pricked the older woman's excitement by the way her voice deflated in her next response.

"It was just an idea."

"Sorry."

"Don't be sorry. Maybe next time. Is Marcel around?"

"No. He's in New York on a video shoot. I can give you his number, though." Diana waited while Camille searched for a pen and then gave her Marcel's phone number.

After they hung up, she thought about what the older woman had said, mainly because it closely mirrored her grandmother's nightly spiel.

Everyone seemed to think she didn't know how to let her hair down and that she worked too hard. Okay, maybe the latter was true, but what choice did she have? She knew how to have fun if she really wanted to . . . sort of. She sighed. Who was she trying to kid?

Today at lunch the rumor mill was in full swing. Marcel's flight up with Nora had all the women practically buzzing and waging bets.

Diana ignored them.

In all, it was an exhausting day and she couldn't wait to get out of there. No sooner had she slid her purse strap over her shoulder to leave than she heard Solomon calling her name.

"Diana. Thank God you're still here." He stopped in front of her desk. "I need a favor. A big favor."

Not now. I just want to go home. She sighed but managed a buoyant smile. "Sure. What can I do for you?"

"I just got a call from Marcel's housekeeper,

Juanita. She's had some type of family emergency and can't get over to his house to feed Brandy."

Diana drew in a breath.

"I would do it," he rushed on. "But I have a flight to catch and there's no one else I can ask on such short notice."

"I don't know," Diana hedged. "I have this thing about dogs."

Solomon came around her desk and took her by the hand. "Please. Brandy is a sweetheart, really. She wouldn't hurt a fly."

"She's a Doberman pinscher."

"A baby."

She frowned. "I thought she was four years old."

"Well." He smiled slyly. "She's young at heart."

"I don't think so." Diana shook her head. Her fear of dogs was no laughing matter. "You're going to have to get someone else."

Solomon dropped to one knee and pressed her hand against his chest. "Please. You have to do this for me . . . for Marcel. You know he loves that dog."

Diana shook her head as she pulled her hand away and then gathered her things. "No. I draw the line at dogs."

Solomon jumped back onto his feet and trailed after her as she headed toward the elevators.

"C'mon. You know as well as I do that Marcel doesn't trust too many people in his house."

"No." Her stride quickened.

"Diana, please don't make me beg."

She pressed for the elevator, smiled at the other associates crowded around, and then turned to face him. "You *are* begging. Where is his personal assistant, Wayne?"

"He's in New York with Marcel. Please do this—for me." He placed his hands together in prayer. "I'll owe you one—big time."

"Charlie?"

"New York."

His pleading gaze rattled her resolve and she couldn't believe that she was actually contemplating doing this for him.

Sensing a victory, he looped an arm around her shoulder and drew her away from the elevator and from curious eyes. "All you have to do is put some food in her dish and let her outside for a few minutes."

"And pick up after her."

"Well, the lawn guy can take care of that later. I don't want to put you out too much."

"Gee, thanks."

He reached into his pants pocket and withdrew a small set of keys. "So, you'll do it?"

"Do I have a choice?"

Solomon uncharacteristically planted a kiss on her cheek. "Marcel's right. You're the best."

Diana blinked. "He said that?"

He handed her a silver key and jotted down the house security code. "All the time."

Dealing with new artists had a way of testing Marcel's patience. It amazed him how this Generation Y constantly wanted something for nothing. He usually didn't supervise video shoots or track recordings, but this new group with their excessive partying and destructive behavior were forcing him to reevaluate keeping them on the label.

They were a talented group, but business was business. Since Nora was the one who discovered the group, she tagged along.

During Marcel's downtime, his mind kept wandering to Diana and the weird silent treatment she gave him. He didn't usually have such a hard time figuring women out, but Diana puzzled him.

What drove her so hard and why was she pushing him away when all he wanted to do was help?

"You're zoning out on me again."

Nora's aggravated voice sliced through his thoughts and pulled him back to the present. Inches from the video director, Marcel sat in his own customized chair with his name scrolled across the back and wondered what the hell Nora was complaining about now. "Is there any way we can talk about your expense reports when we're back at the office?" he asked.

She looked put out, but managed to give him a strained smile. "Didn't you get a chance to go over the numbers I left with Diana a couple of weeks ago?"

"Not yet, but Diana mentioned you had a few questionable requests on it."

"Does that mean I have to get her approval or yours?"

At her sarcastic tone, his gaze jerked up to hers. "I'm not in the mood for this, Nora. Your band here is costing me money. Money I'm not at all sure we're going to be able to recoup."

She sighed. "I know they're rough around the edges, but they're rappers. They're from the streets."

"What are you talking about? Two of them went to Ivy League schools. There's nothing hard core about that."

"Then they're trying to create an image in order to be taken seriously in this genre."

He tossed up his hands. "Are you going to have an excuse for everything?"

Another strained smile. "That depends on whether you're ever going to cut me some slack."

He frowned as he stared at her. "Why are you making this personal? This is business. Your band is out of control. We've spent two weeks on a video that was slated for two days. I have a problem with that—a serious problem. The last thing I want to hear is you asking me to spend even more money on them."

"They're stars. You've heard their music," she defended.

"Talent doesn't impress me as much as bankability. You should know that."

Nora conceded his point, but she wasn't too happy over the whole situation. The Delinquents were her first band signed to the label and she desperately wanted to make them a hit. Their success meant her success and would prove once and for all that she belonged at T&B Entertainment.

However, working beside one of the hottest men in the business was proving to be quite a distraction. Every woman at the company, whether she admitted it or not, wanted to be the one to tame Casanova Brown. Nora was no exception.

So far she wasn't making any headway, but they were going to be in New York for at least another day. She'd managed to snag him for a "business" dinner, and she had every intention of having Marcel for dessert, as well.

Ten

Parked outside her boss's sprawling estate, Diana took a few minutes to question her sanity. This wasn't the first time she'd been to Marcel's home. Usually when she had to make a pit stop here, someone was here to control the dog.

Why in the world did she agree to do this when she was terrified of dogs? Then again, Solomon Bassett could sell a blind man a set of Braille-less encyclopedias.

"Just go in there and get it over with," she coached herself, but made no move for the door. Closing her eyes, she exhaled a long breath. At this rate, both she and the dog would die of starvation.

"Brandy is just a baby," she said, quoting Solomon. Maybe if she said the lie enough times she'd start to believe it. After ten minutes, she ditched that idea, too.

She started up the car. Someone else would have to do this. There was just no way she could conquer this fear. Retrieving her cell phone, she dialed Marcel's cell from memory.

Marcel answered on the first ring.

"You're going have to get someone else to feed your dog. I can't do it," she said with more anger than she intended.

"Diana?"

"Yes, it's me." She swallowed.

"What do you mean you can't feed Brandy? Where is Juanita?"

"Family emergency. Solomon asked me to feed Brandy, but I'm terrified of dogs," she rambled on.

Marcel sighed. "Okay, calm down. Let me think."

Diana did as he instructed, while guilt trickled down her spine. What did she expect him to do when he was in New York?

On the other side of the line, she heard megaphones and music playing. He was still working. "Look, I know this is short notice, but I can't get the image of being mauled to death out of my head."

"By Brandy?" He laughed. "I promise you, she wouldn't hurt a fly. You have to believe me on that."

"I'm sorry," she repeated, starting the car. "But I can't do it."

Marcel's frustration seeped through the line. "We can't let her starve."

"I'm not suggesting that. It's just . . . well, I had a bad experience with a dog once."

"You were bitten?" His voice filled with instant concern.

His concern was probably manufactured to calm her down—and it was working. "When I was a teenager, my grandmother had a neighbor with a rottweiler."

"Uh-huh."

"Well, his name was Killer, of all things. And he was constantly barking and growling at everyone that walked past. I felt safe as long as he was behind the fence."

"Don't tell me. He escaped?" Marcel guessed.

"Dug a hole and crawled out. I swear he must have chased me ten blocks."

"Did he bite you?"

"Bite me? He couldn't catch me," she deadpanned. "When the dust cleared my grandmother insisted I join the track team in high school."

Marcel laughed. "Okay, then you can do this. If you want, I can even stay on the phone with you while you go into the house."

"What are you supposed to do over the phone?"

"I don't know." He sighed. "Give support?"

She shook her head. "Your dog needs to eat and I'm being silly."

"Well, I'd appreciate it if you could feed her. First thing in the morning I can see if I can find someone else to take care of her. Who knows, Juanita might be finished dealing with her emergency."

She agreed, but her heart was already beginning to pound hard. "Are you sure she's not going to attack me?"

"Trust me," he said. "I wouldn't lie to you."

Believing him, she drew a deep breath. "Okay, I'll go in there." *What the hell am I saying?*

"Do you need me to stay on the phone with you?"

"Nah, I think I can handle it." *Someone shut me up.*

After a long pause he asked, "Are you sure?"

Another lengthy silence stretched between them before she shut off the engine.

"Diana?"

"Yeah, I'm sure. I'll call you back if there's a problem." She quickly ended the call before she wound up promising to adopt the damn dog.

A few minutes later, she stood outside Marcel's front door, rubbing her sweaty palms against her slacks. "He promised she wouldn't hurt you. He wouldn't lie." Though a part of her still believed prayers fell on deaf ears, she prayed anyway.

She extracted the house key and the security code from her purse. "Just be calm, cool, and collected," she coached herself. "Dogs can sense fear."

She slipped the key into the lock, but it took her another moment to try and enter the premises. Determination instead of courage came to her rescue and she finally pushed open the door.

Once inside, she quickly found the alarm system's keypad where she nervously entered the pass code. *So far so good.* Diana breathed in a little easier, but when she turned away from the wall, her heart plummeted to her toes.

Brandy's coal-black eyes glittered as she stared at the intruder.

Diana tried not to stare pointedly into the dog's almond-shaped eyes. She read somewhere that aggressive dogs found that threatening. Slowly, her gaze slid down Brandy's slick, solid black coat, and then the rust markings on her head, chest, and legs.

A baby, my ass.

Brandy cocked her head as if she was confused by Diana's presence.

Diana swallowed, but a lump of fear remained

lodged in her throat. "H-hello there." She forced a smile, but felt silly when the dog just continued to stare.

"Okay, I'm going to, uh, get you some food and let you run around outside for a little bit. Would you like that?"

Woof!

Diana jumped and nearly started crying. *Stay calm.* "I can't stay calm." *Yes, you can.* Arguing with herself was definitely a sign that she was indeed losing her marbles.

Brandy cocked her head in the other direction and then sat back on her haunches.

This had to be a good sign, Diana decided, and relaxed long enough for her lungs to start working again. Familiar with the house's layout, she realized she had to work her way around the dog in order to make it to the kitchen or even to the back door.

When her cell phone rang from inside her purse, she jumped and Brandy barked again. Diana's hand quickly covered her heart as if the act would prevent it from leaping out of her chest cavity.

Brandy's barking grew louder with each ring of the phone, but Diana was too nervous to reach for the thing and shut it off. If she died now, how long would it take for someone to wrestle her lifeless body from this *baby's* ferocious mouth?

To her relief, the phone stopped ringing and Brandy lowered back onto her haunches.

"Okay, I'm going to the kitchen now," she said, but was really asking for permission.

Brandy just watched her.

Diana extended one leg and took her first step.

When nothing happened, she was encouraged to take another. At this rate, she'd make it to the kitchen by Christmas. The fact the dog hadn't attacked her yet should have relaxed her, but logic never quite sounded like logic at times like these.

Easing next to the dog, she was grateful that her knocking knees didn't set off another barking frenzy or worse—a violent attack.

However, she didn't know what to think when Brandy turned and quietly trotted behind her to the back door. Diana unlocked and slid the glass door open and Brandy crossed the threshold hardly sparing Diana a glance.

Diana closed the door and almost collapsed into a heap on the floor. Instead, she hurried into the kitchen and quickly prepared the dog's dinner and refilled the water pail. "So far so good," she mumbled under her breath, and went to let the dog back inside.

Brandy jetted inside and made a beeline straight into the kitchen as if she knew what would be waiting for her.

Diana rushed to relock the glass door and was about to head back toward the front door when she stepped on a squeaky toy and bent to pick it up.

That was her first mistake.

Marcel couldn't sit still. His conversation with Diana had him more than a little concerned. Mostly, he didn't understand why she'd agreed to feed Brandy in the first place. It was either courageous or stupid. He wasn't sure which.

He dialed her cell phone again and frowned when he didn't get an answer.

"What's wrong?" Nora asked, rejoining him and handing him a steaming cup of coffee.

"Nothing, I hope." He accepted the offered cup, but couldn't pull his thoughts away from Diana. "Look, you don't mind just having dinner with Solomon tonight, do you?"

She straightened in alarm. "Solomon? I didn't know he was joining us."

"Well, we had some business to discuss and I didn't see anything wrong with trying to kill two birds with one stone. But now I think I need to get back home."

"What? Why?"

"At the moment, I'm a little concerned about my secretary."

"Diana?"

"Yeah. She went to feed Brandy today and she's terrified of dogs." A small laugh escaped him.

Nora shrugged. "So? She's a big girl."

He shrugged as well. "She's not answering her cell phone so I'm worried."

"I don't see what the big deal is," she argued. "Just send someone over to check on her."

Marcel frowned. "Why are you getting so worked up? I've been up here for two weeks. The director promised he'd wrap this shoot by tonight. There's no reason for me to stay."

"But I needed to talk with you."

"You know," he said, crossing his arms, "Solomon is vice president of the company. He's more than capable of handling whatever issue you might have." He walked away, shaking his head.

Thwarting Nora's cat-and-mouse games was a challenge at times . . . but fun. How many times had he told her he made it a policy not to get involved with his employees? He frowned as Charlie opened the door to his limousine. If that was true, then why was he racing back to Atlanta to see Diana Guy?

Eleven

Tim and Caleb stopped by Diana's apartment only to find a worried Louisa.

At six four, Caleb was often hailed as a take-charge kind of guy. In no time, he calmed Lou down enough for her to tell them the last time she'd talked to Diana.

When Tim heard Diana had left her office eight hours ago, he, too, grew concerned. It wasn't like Diana not to check in. She was always reliable, dependable, and responsible. Something had to have happened.

"Maybe we should call the police," Tim suggested.

Lou unfolded her wrinkled tissue and dabbed her eyes dry. "I've already done that. They left here an hour ago, but they said there was nothing they could do until she'd been missing for twenty-four hours."

"Maybe she's out with some of her girlfriends from the job," Caleb suggested.

"She doesn't have girlfriends," Lou said.

"None?"

"None," Lou and Tim answered in unison.

Caleb fell silent as he digested that information. His new career in international sales and marketing kept him out of town so he didn't know Diana as well as his partner.

"Then let's pile in the car and retrace her steps," Caleb said. "That's gotta be better than sitting around twirling our thumbs."

"What if she calls?" Lou asked, her eyes filling with tears.

"She's right," Tim said. "Someone should be here if she does call."

Caleb nodded. "All right. You two stay here and I'll go. She still works for T&B Entertainment, right?"

Lou jumped to her feet and wrapped her short arms around the man she often called a gentle giant. "Oh, thank you. I'll feel so much better knowing someone is actually out there looking for her."

Caleb looped his large arms around her as well and gave her an affectionate squeeze. "I'll bring her back home."

Marcel wasn't able to leave New York immediately. But he left his personal assistant, Fred, behind to tidy up any loose ends. By the time his private jet touched down just after midnight he was exhausted. Dreams of a much-needed vacation drifted lazily across his mind.

He fell asleep in the limo, with dreams of the beautiful island of Bermuda seducing him with its white sandy beaches, to dance the night away with bronzed beauties.

"Sir, were you expecting someone tonight?" Charlie's voice filtered through the speaker and jarred him from his deep sleep.

"What?"

"There's a car here."

Frowning, Marcel pried his eyes open and rolled down his window. At the sight of Diana's car, he was instantly alert.

Before the limo rolled to a complete stop, Marcel was out of the vehicle and racing toward the front door. "Diana," he shouted as the door banged open.

Brandy's bark resonated from upstairs and he quickly headed in that direction. Halfway up, he discovered a purse and its contents scattered across the stairs.

"What in the hell?" He looked up and slowly continued on. "Diana?"

"Sir, is there a problem?" Charlie asked from the front door.

"I'll know in a minute."

Brandy bounded out of a bedroom, a toy squeaking loudly from between her teeth.

"Hey, girl. How are you doing?" He walked up to her and scratched behind her ears. "Where's Diana?"

Brandy dropped her toy and cocked her head.

"Show me where the nice lady is," he said.

Like a good girl, Brandy turned around and went back into the bedroom.

Marcel followed and frowned when she'd stopped in front of a closet, but he cautiously went to it and opened the door.

At the sudden scream, Marcel jumped back and Brandy barked.

"Keep her away from me," Diana yelled and uncurled from the closet floor to slam the door closed again.

It took Marcel a second to process what he'd just seen: his secretary transformed into a hysterical crazy woman. "Diana?"

"I mean it, Marcel. Make her go away."

He looked down at Brandy, who lifted hurtful eyes toward him. "Sorry, girl. Go on downstairs."

Brandy hung her head and padded out of the room.

Marcel walked over to the bedroom door and closed it. "All right, Diana. She's gone." He heard some rustling before the closet door squeaked open.

"Are you sure she's gone?"

He moved back to the closet and the utter terror on her face squeezed his heart. "She's downstairs. My God, how long have you been in there?"

"I'm not sure." Diana timidly eased out of the closet, looking nothing like his well-put-together secretary, but more like a tousled mess with dazed eyes.

There was a soft knock on the door. "Sir, is everything all right?"

"Yes, Charlie. Everything is fine," Marcel called out. "Ms. Guy was just frightened. She's going to be just fine."

"Yes, sir."

Marcel draped his arm around Diana and pulled her close. "Come over here and sit down," he said, leading her over to the room's king-size bed.

Once she was settled, he was at a loss for what he should do next. "Uh, can I get you something? Do you need a doctor or anything?"

Diana took several breaths, seemingly to calm herself down before being able to focus on him. Then, she came up swinging. "You said that she wouldn't attack me," she screamed, swatting his arms, chest, and whatever else her hands landed on. "You lied."

"What? Wait! Whoa!" Marcel tried to dodge out of the way, but was unsuccessful. Instead, he waited for her to get it all out, which, thank heavens, didn't take long.

"Do you know how terrified I was?" She slumped back onto the bed. "I thought I was going to die in that closet."

The dark angry flush to Diana's cheeks, the bright sparkle in her eyes, and the wild tussle of her hair gave his prim and proper secretary the look of a seductive siren, which struck a chord with him. A nice chord.

He cleared his throat and tried to shake the direction of his thoughts. "I think maybe you might have overreacted."

"Overreacted!" Her eyes widened. "You've got to be kidding. Your *baby* chased me around the entire house barking and nipping at my heels."

Marcel frowned. "Brandy?"

"No, Lassie. Of course, Brandy. She was going to rip me to shreds."

"Brandy?"

"Yes, Brandy. Will you stop asking that?"

"I'm sorry, but it just doesn't sound like something she would do."

"What? You think I'm making this up or something?" Her anger started refueling itself.

He held up his hands. "No, no. I'm not saying that. It's just—"

"Then what are you saying?" Her hands jabbed at her hips.

Marcel took a deep breath while trying to figure

out another way to handle this. "Why don't you just tell me what happened?"

Reining in her temper, Diana told him everything that had transpired after their call.

"You picked up one of her toys?" He stopped her in the middle of her story.

She shrugged. "It was lying in the middle of the floor."

A smile wobbled at the corners of his lips. "Tell me," he said, crossing his arms. "When she was chasing you throughout the house, did you still have the toy in your hand?"

Diana frowned. "I don't know. I guess so."

"That explains it." Marcel laughed. "She wasn't attacking you. She was playing."

His laughter deepened but Diana just glared at him. "Do I look like I'm amused?"

"Ah, no." All humor evaporated from his face. "You look sort of pissed."

"That's because I am." She stood up from the bed again. "Don't ever ask me to do this again. And I'm shooting Solomon on sight." Storming past him, she went back to the closet and then walked around. "What did I do with my purse?"

"You dropped it on the stairs," he said, walking behind her as she headed out of the bedroom.

"Figures. I'm out of here." She jerked open the door, but then screamed, slammed it, and leaped against Marcel.

His body instantly became alert with the cute bundle enfolded in his arms. He was suddenly aware of the soft fragrance in her hair and the sweet scent of vanilla on her skin. She couldn't possibly know how sexy she looked right now. "What is it?" he asked, his heart slamming against his rib cage.

"She's outside the door."

"Who?"

"Your dog!"

Her eyes darkened to sparkling jewels again and Marcel wondered what she would do if he kissed her right now. It was a stupid and wild idea that appealed and concerned him. "I'll go put her up," he said, but struggled to pull his gaze away from her.

Diana moved away from the door while Marcel waltzed past her and out of the door as she struggled to bring her breathing back to normal. For a moment there, she wasn't sure if her heart was pounding because of the dog or how Marcel had looked at her.

Being near Marcel often clouded her thinking and her ability to process rational thought became an arduous chore, but he could have sworn there was something more to the way he'd just looked at her. In fact, she couldn't remember him ever looking at her like that.

"You're imagining things," she said, shaking her head. But a part of her wasn't so sure.

Twelve

While Marcel led Brandy out to the dog run, he couldn't stop the smile that stretched across his face. Damned if he understood why he found Diana's anger such a turn-on—but he did.

Sliding open the back door, he gave Brandy an affectionate scratch behind the ear before she trotted out.

"Is there anything else I can do for you, sir?" Charlie asked, joining him in the living room.

Marcel glanced at his watch. It was nearly one A.M. "No, I'm good. You can head home."

"Thank you, sir," Charlie said, but didn't leave.

"Something else on your mind?"

Charlie smiled. "I was just wondering if Ms. Guy would be needing a lift or an escort home."

Marcel's lazy smile diminished when he suddenly remembered Charlie and Diana's curious friendship. "I believe I can see to it that she makes it home."

Charlie raised an inquisitive brow, but he didn't question Marcel. "Yes, sir."

Marcel's gaze narrowed in suspicion as he followed Charlie toward the front door. Surely if something was truly going on between the driver and his secretary the man would've protested more about her being left alone with him.

Charlie stopped a few feet from the front door and pivoted around to face Marcel. "If I may, sir?"

Marcel's heart sank. "What is it, Charlie?"

Charlie looked unsure of himself. "About Ms. Guy," he began.

"What about her?" Marcel asked almost defensively.

Charlie hesitated. "She's not like the other women you tend to . . . date."

Surprised, Marcel arched his brows. "Oh?"

Charlie swallowed. "Yes, she's, uh, special."

With his good humor finally returning, Marcel laughed and crossed his arms. "I'm not sure I understand what you're getting at."

"No disrespect, sir," Charlie said with an awkward grin. "But I believe you do."

Marcel's smile froze and the laugh he forced out cracked under pressure. "I guess maybe I do," he finally said. "But, uh, there's just one problem, Charlie. I'm not dating Diana. She's my secretary. I have a rule about dating employees, remember?"

Charlie remained unmoved by his candor. "I know you as Casanova Brown as well, sir. And for him, rules have been known to be broken."

* * *

Diana settled back on the bed and picked up the bedside phone to call home. Her grandmother was undoubtedly out of her mind with worry.

After she'd dialed the number, she wasn't even sure the line rang once before Louisa's shaky voice answered.

"Hey, Nana. It's me. And yes, I'm fine."

"Oh, thank God," Louisa sighed, and then immediately tore a chunk out of Diana's hide. "Why didn't you call? Do you know how worried I've been?"

"I'm sorry," Diana said and quickly informed her of what she'd been through that evening.

"Why on earth would you agree to feed the man's dog when you're—"

"I know, I know. I wasn't thinking right. And Lord knows I've learned my lesson."

"Well, Caleb is out looking for you," Louisa said. "I'll call him and tell him you're all right."

"Thanks, Nana. I'll be home soon."

"Well, you can take your time, dear. Now that I know where you are, I can get some sleep. Oh, tell Marcel I said hi."

"You've got the wrong idea, Nana."

"Don't take away my dreams, Diana."

Sighing, Diana ended the call. She could already feel exhaustion seeping into her bones.

She looked around and for the first time took in the room's excessive extravagance: beautiful paintings, expensive colored glass vases, and a plasma television. "Must be nice."

What was taking Marcel so long, she wondered. She stood up from the bed and walked over to the door. She reached for the knob, but then thought she should at least check to make sure he and Brandy weren't on the other side ready to pull some horrible joke on her.

She leaned over and pressed her ear against the door. In the next second, it flew open and smashed her back against the wall.

"Di—"

"Ooww!"

Marcel pulled the door and peeked around it. "Oh, I'm so sorry." He closed the door and went to her. "Are you all right?"

She held up a hand to keep him back, but when her other hand touched her throbbing nose, she howled in pain.

"Di?"

"What are you trying to do, kill me?" She inched away from the wall and returned to the bed. "I don't know who's worse, you or the dog."

Marcel followed her, trying to get a good look at what he'd done. "I'll go get you some ice."

Before she could stop him, he rushed out. "I need to get out of here," she said, pulling herself off the bed. "Enough is enough."

Marching out of the room, Diana had no intention of waiting for ice.

At the stairs, she saw her purse and its contents sprawled everywhere. "Just great." She walked down and started picking up her things.

Marcel returned and raced up to her. "Hey, I'll get that for you."

Diana crammed what she had into her purse and then sat on the stairs. If she wasn't so mad, she was sure she would start crying.

"Come here," he said, sitting next to her.

She eyed him wearily.

"Trust me."

"You're kidding, right?"

Marcel exhaled. "Please."

His soft puppy dog look was extremely effective, she realized as she inched closer.

"Thank you." He rewarded her with a breathtaking smile. "Now tilt your head back."

She did as he said and sighed in relief when he pressed a cool compress against the bridge of her nose.

"I take it you like that." He chuckled.

"Ooh, that feels good." She stretched back on the stairs. "I almost want to forgive you for nearly breaking it in the first place."

"You're too gracious."

She smiled and kept her eyes closed. Though she was enjoying the soothing feeling from the ice, Diana was quite aware of the heat generating from him as well. Lying so close, she relished the way the faint scent of his cologne tickled her nose.

"Is there anything else I can get for you?" he asked, his minty breath drifting across the shell of her ear.

She swallowed hard and slowly shook her head.

"Surely, you don't want to lie on the stairs like this?"

"I'm fine. I'm leaving anyway."

"I better move you back to the bed."

"That won't be—"

His arms swooped beneath her body and lifted her.

Diana's eyes flew open as she finally removed the compress from her nose. Pretending that she didn't feel a bolt of electricity throughout her body while cradled in his arms was nearly impossible. "Mr. Taylor—"

"We're back to Mr. Taylor again?" he asked, carrying her into the spare bedroom.

Was that annoyance she heard in his tone? What the hell was he annoyed about? She was the one with the day from hell. "Marcel, if you could please put me down. I don't need to lie on the bed," she finished just as he placed her on the cream and gold comforter. "Besides, I'm starting to feel much better," she added.

Marcel's expression soured as he reached up and gently tweaked her nose.

"Ooww!"

"Yeah, much better." He chuckled.

"Maybe it's broken," she said with sudden concern.

"If you'd let me get a good look at it."

"No!"

He stood up and folded his arms. "Now, Diana, I thought you were many things, but I never would've thought you were a coward."

"Finding me at the bottom of a closet should have been your first hint."

He stared at her. "Good point. Do you want to go to the emergency room?"

She placed the compress back against her nose and wondered if she really thought the thing was broken. "No. I guess not." She eased back against the bed's pillows. "I'll just lie here until it stops throbbing."

He rewarded her with another beautiful smile. "Good girl," he said, ruffling her hair.

"Stop that. I'm not a dog, you know."

He actually managed to look contrite. "Sorry."

Diana smiled. "It's all right." Then her eyes grew wide when he walked around to the other side and climbed onto the bed to lie next to her.

"Just in case I didn't say it earlier, thank you. It was very courageous of you to try to take care of Brandy with your phobia."

She shrugged. "I wouldn't necessarily call it a phobia."

He chuckled and caused the bed to vibrate gently beneath her. An image of him reaching over and unbuttoning her blouse flashed through her head. As a result a sweet tingle shot through her body and curled her toes.

"Diana?"

"Huh, what?"

He frowned. "I asked you what you would call your fear."

She blinked and shook the R-rated thoughts from her head. "I don't know. Crazy, I suppose."

Another chuckle, another jiggle of the mattress.

After a while the room grew loud with silence. Diana kept her eyes closed and concentrated on trying not to think about just how close their bodies were at that moment.

"Mind if I ask you a personal question?" Marcel asked.

"Yes."

"All right, I'll ask it anyway."

"Surprise, surprise."

"Is there anyone special in your life?"

Diana's eyes flew open as she lowered the compress. "I fail to see how that's any of your business." She sat up.

Marcel followed suit. "I realize I'm prying."

"But?"

"There's no but. I'm just curious. Seems to me any man would be happy to have you."

"I'm leaving."

Before she could pull away, Marcel's electrifying touch restrained her. "Look, I'm sorry. You're right. None of this is any of my business."

It wasn't the words so much as the tone that kept her frozen on the bed. Frankly, she didn't think he was sorry at all, but his underlying and seductive baritone instantly caused her pulse to quicken and her head to fill with erotic images.

"It's okay," she said in a shaky whisper. "But I really do need to get going."

"You know you're more than welcome to stay."

Her gaze jerked to him. "Stay?"

He shrugged. "It's late and with seventeen bedrooms, there's plenty of space."

Again, the words were innocent, but the tone wasn't. Was this the way the infamous Casanova Brown worked his magic?

"It's a generous offer—"

"But?"

"But I think it's inappropriate."

Marcel laughed and the bed bounced wonderfully beneath her.

"Don't tell me you're afraid to be alone with me in a twenty-five-thousand-square-foot house."

"We're only three inches apart right now," she said.

His gaze turned somber as it locked onto hers. "Don't you feel safe with me?"

That tone again. "With you, yes. From you is a different story."

He blinked in surprise, turned, and stood from

the bed. "My reputation as Casanova Brown is more urban legend than fact," he said defensively.

"So you haven't slept with a lot of women?"

He stalled as if he just realized he'd backed into a corner. "I've had a few relationships."

Diana crossed her arms. "How many?"

He blinked again, and looked like a deer caught in headlights.

"Urban legend, right."

"Okay, you're right. I've overindulged in the past. But I don't attack women in the middle of the night. I'm more than capable of being around a good-looking woman without having to jump her bones."

Good-looking? Diana's hand instantly flew up to her mussed hair. She undoubtedly looked as if she'd been in a train wreck.

"And what about you?" he asked, going on the attack. "How many men have you had sex with?"

Diana jumped from the bed. "That is none of your business!"

"Ah, the good old double standard." Marcel smirked. "Maybe I should be the one worried about being alone with you."

"That's ridiculous," she huffed, tossing the compress on the nightstand and then storming toward the door.

"Come on. Give me a hint. Ten, fifteen, twenty?"

"Give me a break," she said, rolling her eyes.

Marcel blocked her exit. "Twenty-two? And I mean all forms of sex."

She stabbed him with an angry glare. "It's none of your business!"

"Twenty-five?"

"You're crazy."

"Thirty-five?"

"One," she yelled, her face burning with indignation.

Marcel flashed her a wide victorious grin. "See, now, that wasn't so bad, was it?"

Thirteen

Marcel's lazy gaze drifted down Diana's reddening face to that cute figure she kept trying to hide. "Just one, eh?"

Diana stormed around Marcel.

"Wait. Where are you going?" Marcel asked, chasing behind her.

"Home." She stomped down the stairs.

"Oh, come on. Surely you're not mad because you told me how many men you've been with?"

She didn't respond.

"It's nothing to be ashamed of."

Diana stopped in the middle of the staircase, causing Marcel to nearly collide into her.

"Who said anything about being ashamed?"

He blinked. "No one. By the way you're reacting, I thought—"

"Well, you thought wrong," she declared. "I chose the right person to lose my virginity to. He was sweet, kind, giving." Her gaze narrowed on him. "...And monogamous."

Marcel lifted his chin after the verbal blow. "Yeah? So where did you meet this clown?"

Diana smiled. "Georgia State University. We were college sweethearts."

"Is that right?" Marcel crossed his arms, disliking the image of Diana and some nameless guy flashing in his head. "Well, here's a news flash: no man is monogamous during college. I don't even think it's genetically possible."

Diana rolled her eyes and continued to descend the stairs. "I'm sure that all the college jocks you hung out with got off trying to see how many women they could score, but take my word for it, there's another breed of men who actually believe in the one man, one woman theory."

"This might surprise you, Ms. Guy, but I also believe in the theory," he said and enjoyed wiping the superior smirk off her face.

He took the lead down the staircase. "Now, I might have had my fun in the past, but that doesn't mean that I don't want to settle down and raise a family. On the contrary."

A disbelieving Diana followed him to a spacious entertainment room, complete with pool table, old pinball machines, jukebox, and stocked bar. "When did this miracle take place?" she asked.

He shrugged. "I've always believed it. Want a drink?"

"I don't believe you. No, thanks to the drink."

"Come on. After the day you had, you deserve one." He waltzed behind the bar.

"Ain't that the truth?" She slumped onto a bar stool and caught her reflection in the mirror behind him. "Oh, my God. I look horrible." She immediately tried to smooth down her hair.

Marcel smiled as he set two glasses down on the counter. "Actually, I like it. It has that fresh-out-of-bed look I love so much."

She rolled her eyes. "You would say something like that."

Marcel laughed. "You know, Di. I'm starting to believe you don't like me."

She glanced away and shrugged. "I wouldn't say that . . . exactly."

Marcel's brows rose with amusement. "Not exactly? You sure do know how to hurt a man."

"I'm not trying to hurt you. It's just that after two years of ordering morning-after flowers, tons of Godiva chocolates, and mailing little trinkets for just about everyone in your little black book, I'm sort of skeptical about all of this."

Marcel shrugged. "I see your point." He gave each glass a few cubes of ice. "How about rum and Coke?"

"Fine."

"My whole point is that there comes a time in every man's life when he has to make a few decisions. And I think that time has finally come for me."

Diana's dubious gaze remained glued on him.

He smiled and pushed her glass toward her. "You're worse than Solomon when I told him."

"Well, if you're serious, then I applaud you." She sipped her drink.

Marcel leaned across the bar with his own drink in hand. "If you don't mind my asking, whatever happened to your college lover boy?"

She studied him as if weighing whether she should answer. "Personality conflict."

"That is just about as vague as irreconcilable differences. It doesn't tell me anything."

She smiled. "Ian was what you might call a control freak. Not only in business but in our private lives as well. My own sense of independence couldn't deal with that."

Marcel frowned. "You dated someone named Ian?" He gulped down a third of his drink before adding, "That might have been your first mistake."

"What's wrong with his name?"

Marcel shrugged. "It's not exactly a manly name, is it?"

"And Marcel is? Sounds like you should have your own fashion line or something. What about the women you date? Last year you actually dated a black woman named Buffy. Buffy!"

"Actually, it was her stage name," he said.

"Oh? She was a singer?"

"Close. A stripper."

Diana shook her head. "Should've known."

Marcel's grin slid wider. "What did this *Ian* do for a living?"

"He's in politics. Last I heard he's a senator from Rhode Island."

"A monogamous politician? Sounds like an oxymoron to me."

"Everyone's a cynic."

They laughed.

Diana didn't know whether it was the company or the much-needed drink that relaxed her, but she did know that she was beginning to enjoy this rather candid and intimate discussion with her boss.

"Now you tell me something about one of your relationships. Not a one-night stand, but an actual relationship. Why didn't it work out?"

Marcel sucked in a deep breath and rolled his eyes back as if he had to dust off a very old memory chip. "All right, my last real relationship was almost three years ago. Her name was Kelly. She was forty-two—"

"An older woman?"

"Yeah, but she had the body of a twenty-five-year-old."

Why did I ask? "Continue."

"Well, we met at a ski resort in Aspen, had a ball for about a month, and then it ended."

"Why?"

He shrugged. "Turned out that she was still married to some big-shot banker. She decided she wanted to give her marriage another shot and left me in the cold."

"She dumped you?" she asked, dumbfounded.

"What? I've had a broken heart before. A few times actually."

Just like that, Marcel Taylor transformed from a business mogul with a wild and infamous reputation to a real human being with a history of pain and heartache.

"I guess I had you figured wrong," Diana said, finishing her drink. "I thought you were just a 'love 'em and leave 'em' kind of guy."

He fixed them another drink. "I'm not completely innocent of those charges."

Diana held up her hand. "I was just starting to like you. Don't ruin it."

"You got it." He held up his glass and clinked it against Diana's.

Their talk moved away from the bar and into the living room. To Diana's amazement and dismay, Marcel broke out photo albums of dogs. The way he carried on, one would have thought he was boasting about real children. Diana knew the alcohol was kicking in when she started thinking the dogs were actually cute.

"I'm probably overcompensating for the fact I was never allowed to have animals when I was growing up. My father's edict was if it couldn't make a sandwich or wipe its own butt, it couldn't live in his house."

Diana laughed, having no trouble imagining Donald Taylor saying just that. "I owned a goldfish once," she admitted, closing the photo album.

"Oh?" Marcel asked, sipping from his fourth drink.

"Yeah." She thought back and laughed. "You should have seen me. I was eight years old and tickled pink that I had something of my very own to take care of. I named him Henry. Every morning I'd wake up and feed him, when I came home from school I fed him, and again just before I went to sleep at night."

"You fed him three times a day?"

Diana bobbed her head. "At least. On the weekends more than that."

"I'm almost afraid to hear what happened."

"I woke up the morning of show-and-tell at school and found him floating on his side."

"Were you devastated?"

"No." She lowered her gaze and chuckled again. "I was actually excited that after swimming for so long, Henry was finally taking a nap. Nana was cool. She went along with it and told me that I should take Henry to school on a day when he wasn't so tired. When I came home, Henry was up from his nap. And every three weeks Henry took another nap. I didn't know any better until I was ten."

"You're kidding me." Marcel laughed.

"Nope. Nana had to tell me the truth because after thirty-seven goldfish, the pet store owner refused to sell her another one." Diana doubled over laughing.

"That's horrible. Why didn't she just tell you to stop feeding Henry so much? Or should I say Henries?"

Diana caught her breath. "She did, but I didn't want him starving to death. I ate three meals a day so I thought he should too."

As the early hours crept closer toward dawn, Marcel and Diana continued to laugh and swap stories as though they were old friends at a high school reunion.

With the exception of his childhood friend Ophelia, Marcel hadn't ever felt this comfortable around a woman. Several times he would stop and smile at Diana's fresh-out-of-bed look and could feel himself drawn to her quiet beauty—her cuteness.

The few times she'd caught him staring, he would quickly drop his gaze.

"What is it?" she finally asked. "Do I look that bad?"

"No, no. You look fine," he assured her, but suddenly grew quite fascinated with her mouth. Her lips were still tinted with a fading shade of red and they tempted him with their provocative shape.

Though Diana shared plenty of stories of her childhood, Marcel was aware that there were quite a few gaps. Like, what did her mother pass away from? Why didn't her parents ever marry? And where was her father now?

Diana sighed and smiled at him. "Enough about me. Let's talk about you again."

"Ah, my favorite subject."

She shook her head. "Why do you say things like that? It makes you sound arrogant."

He smiled. "Please, don't hold back. Tell me what you think."

"Sorry," she said, her eyes glossy from the alcohol. "But I think you're a big fake."

"Is that right?"

She nodded and then frowned as if the act hurt her head. "One minute you pretend to be this insatiable playboy who has to be seen at every party in town, and then at work you're this driven workaholic who's a little stingy when it comes to raises. And now I'm learning that you're also this strange homebody whose best girl is a four-year-old Doberman pinscher."

"Stingy when it comes to raises?" Marcel laughed at the realization that his secretary was indeed drunk.

"I want to know," she said, leaning toward him. "Which person is the real Marcel Taylor?"

"All of them," he answered. "Just like you're more than my no-nonsense secretary. You're a woman who has loved and lost, and as a result you avoid the reckless emotion like the plague."

Diana straightened.

"You take on too much and ask for very little. You're scared of dogs and should be arrested if you're ever within fifty feet of a goldfish." He softened the mood by laughing again. "All in all, you're an intriguing woman."

She gave an unladylike snort. "First time I ever heard that."

His hand glided over hers. Its warmth was a welcome comfort.

"You've always intrigued me."

Diana slid her hand from beneath his and frowned at the empty glass in her hand. "I've had too much to drink."

"That's a possibility."

"Is this how you snare women in your web?"

"I don't have to get a woman drunk to spend the night, if that's what you're referring to. Most find me charming. Don't you?"

"No."

"Liar."

She laughed. "Maybe."

"You're still lying."

Releasing a boisterous laugh, Diana eased back against the sofa. "Then I plead the Fifth."

"Smart woman," he said, his laughter blending with hers.

"Okay, I have a serious question," she said.

"Shoot."

"Now, I've read the official press release on how you and Solomon started T&B Entertainment by borrowing the funds from your father and all. But I want to know why. You two were jocks for the most part."

"That's easy. For the women."

"Be serious."

"I am. Women like jocks and musicians. Since we're neither, we figured out a way to be the next best thing. Simple as that."

Diana gave up and rolled her eyes. "Pig."

"Sex is a wonderful thing, Di. Don't let anyone ever tell you otherwise." He just laughed as she slapped his arm.

They continued swapping stories and pouring drinks long after dawn's early light filled the house.

Despite having seventeen bedrooms, both fell asleep on the large sofa, too drunk to really give a damn.

The wild dreams filtering in and out of Diana's head had her feeling good. Damn good in fact.

It had been a long time since her body tingled this way. She felt sexy, desirable, and wanton all at the same time. Did she have Marcel Taylor to thank for that?

She sighed when an image of him flitted into her dreams. He was a beautiful man. Cocky—sure. Arrogant—definitely. But the man had a body for sex, eyes for seduction, and a smile that could steal her soul.

"Mmmm. You smell so good," Marcel whispered before he pressed a kiss against the lobe of her ear.

She giggled and curled away from him.

"Where are you going?" He chuckled and pulled her back. He placed another kiss against the column of her neck and evoked a series of giggles.

His kisses grew persistent and a tidal wave of sensations wiped her out. By the time his hot mouth covered hers, she was writhing beneath him with aching abandonment.

Heaven on earth was all she could think. His lips were like heaven on earth. She took her time and savored every inch of his glorious mouth. Despite the barrier of clothing, Marcel's rock-hard erection rubbed against her feminine entrance.

Diana's legs widened so she could cradle him between them. His hands slid beneath her blouse and took their time during their journey toward her breasts. They were the perfect fit in the palms of his hands and when he gave them a gentle squeeze, he swallowed her resultant whimper.

Something was ringing off in the distance, but

nothing was going to disturb this groove, these glorious emotions, this sweet, sweet dream. However, the ringing wouldn't go away.

Diana pried her lips away from Marcel's to yell, "Will someone please get that?"

"What the hell?" a voice thundered above her.

Diana's eyes jerked open. At the sight of a startled Marcel, she screamed, pushed, kicked, and shoved.

Marcel toppled over and crashed onto the wooden coffee table. His howl of pain succeeded in shutting her up, but when she looked down to see her breasts spilling out of her blouse another wave of panic consumed her.

"Oh, my God. Oh, my God," she screamed.

He stood rubbing his head. "Calm down, and for goodness' sake, please stop hollering like that."

"Do you know what we were doing? What almost happened? Oh, my God. I have to get out of here."

The doorbell rang and Diana recognized what had just saved her from being another notch on Casanova Brown's bedpost.

She buttoned her blouse and looked around the room. "Where are my shoes?"

He searched around. "I don't know. What time is it?"

Diana glanced at her watch but was surprised as she read, "Twelve o'clock."

"P.M?" he asked.

"Apparently." Diana suddenly felt as if Lake Michigan were pressing against her kidneys. "Where is the nearest bathroom?"

Marcel plopped back onto the sofa. "Down the hall on your right."

The doorbell rang again and Marcel picked up

some type of gadget from the end table and spoke into it. "Yeah, who's out there?"

Heading toward the bathroom, Diana stopped in her tracks when a syrupy-sweet feminine voice answered through a house speaker.

"Hey, you're home. It's me, Nora."

Fourteen

Mornings were usually hard for Louisa. Most of the time, it took all of her strength just to climb out of bed. Today, however, she was excited to find out what time Diana actually made it home. Since she hadn't retired until two A.M. waiting for Diana, Louisa hoped that maybe, just maybe, something wonderful might have transpired.

It was a long shot that anything happened between her guarded granddaughter and the handsome bachelor, but Louisa had always been a sucker for romance and a fool for great sex. And her instincts told her that her grandbaby just might have gotten herself a little action with that gorgeous boss of hers.

She slipped into her slippers, donned her housecoat, and hustled out of her bedroom. When she approached Diana's bedroom, she was downright giddy.

"Diana?" She knocked on her door and waited only a second before twisting the knob. "It's me,

Diana." She poked her head through the door and glanced over at the bed. "Empty."

She squealed with delight and even managed to perform a happy dance.

Heavy footsteps rushed down the hall. Startled, she glanced up at a frightened Tim. "Louisa, what's wrong?"

She clapped her hands together. "She's not home."

He exhaled. "I know. I haven't been able to sleep a wink." He rubbed his hands along the crop of his hair before turning around. "I'm about to make some coffee. Want some?"

Louisa rushed to catch up with him. "Aren't you excited?"

"Exhausted would be the word I'd use." His mouth stretched wide during a yawn. "I'm getting too old to stay up all night."

"Well, wait until you reach my age."

"Which is?"

"None of your business." She popped him on the arm and smiled. "Now, where is Caleb?"

"Home, asleep. His stamina isn't what it used to be either."

Louisa giggled at the double entendre. "You're so bad." She sashayed into the kitchen ahead of him where the morning coffee had automatically started brewing. "Can I tempt you with some breakfast?"

"Nah. I better get back so I can take care of my own breadwinner." He joined her in front of the microwave and gave her a kiss on the cheek. "Tell Diana to call me when she gets in."

"You're not curious about what happened last night?"

"Are you kidding? I'm *dying* to get the juicy details, but I'm not asking any questions. If she wants me to know anything, then she'll tell me."

Louisa rolled her eyes. "You're no fun. I, on the other hand, am going to leave no stone unturned. If I think there's the slightest chance that Diana cares for Marcel, then I'm going to do all I can to make sure she gets him."

After easing the pressure on her bladder, Diana did her best to clean up her appearance. All the while, she pretended that it didn't matter that Nora was probably out there in an itty-bitty miniskirt and batting her expensive mink eyelashes.

Now that Diana thought about it, Nora and Marcel probably would make a decent couple. Not only were they both beautiful people, but they also loved and sought out the finer things in life. For example: why would a bachelor with no children need a seventeen-bedroom house?

"It's ridiculous," she mumbled, struggling to pull her hair in a French braid. "I don't know how I even remotely thought that I . . . that I felt . . . Oh, forget it." She jerked open the bathroom door to find Marcel standing there, holding out her shoes.

"I found them."

Diana placed a hand over her heart and wondered wildly just how long he'd been standing there. "Where's Nora?"

"Gone." He leaned against the door frame.

"Gone where?"

"Does it matter?"

Diana shrugged. "I guess not."

He frowned. "So who were you talking to in there?"

"No one." She grabbed her shoes.

"Do you talk to yourself often?"

"I plead the Fifth." She slid on her shoes and flashed him a fake smile before walking around him. "I better get out of here."

"No breakfast?"

"It's lunchtime," she said, returning to the living room.

"Fine. Lunch, then?"

"I would love to but . . ."

Both stopped and turned at the sound of the front door opening and closing. Seconds later, a soft, lyrical voice floated throughout the house. "Marcel, darling?" Diana's narrowed gaze shifted to her boss and her heart broke at seeing his face light up.

"Ophelia? Is that you?" He deserted Diana's side and strode to the front door.

Ophelia? Why did the name seem familiar? "This place is just a regular chick magnet," she mumbled and snatched her purse from the sofa. Before she could make a dramatic exit, Marcel returned with a Beyoncé Knowles look-alike clinging to his waist.

"It's so good to see you," he said and placed a kiss against her forehead.

"I hope you don't mind my using the key you gave me."

"Of course not. That's why I gave it to you."

When Ophelia's beautiful honey-colored gaze lifted to Diana, a cold chill blew across her spine. She'd seen this woman before. Both Marcel and Solomon had a picture of her sitting on their desks.

In the past, Diana had wondered which man the beauty had dated or whether she'd perhaps dated both.

"Oh. Hello." Ophelia smiled. "Marcel, aren't you going to introduce us?"

He blinked. "Of course."

"You know, that's not necessary," Diana interrupted. Her desire to get the hell out of there propelled her to rush past them.

"But, Di—"

"I have to get home and see about my grandmother, anyway." She rushed on to the door.

Marcel left his golden lady to follow her to the door. "Well, I'm sorry that you have to leave."

"I should have left last night." She opened the door. "I guess I'll see you on Monday."

"Yeah. Uh, bright and early." He smiled and looked as if he didn't know what else to say before settling on, "About what happened this morning, or rather afternoon."

Diana's face burned with embarrassment. "Uh, forget it. It was no big deal."

He straightened. "I don't know. It seemed like a big deal twenty minutes ago."

An awkward smile wobbled at the corners of her lips. Why was it so difficult to get out of this man's house? "Look, I admit I freaked for a minute there, but I'm willing to forget the whole thing happened."

He stared at her and slowly nodded his head. "Yeah, I guess that would be the best thing to do. I mean, we were . . . we . . ."

"Had too much to drink," she offered for him.

He slid his hands into his pants pockets. "Yeah. We did."

His gaze softened as it roamed over her face.

Then again, it was probably her imagination again. "Bye." She turned away and headed to her car. It was just in time, too, because she was seconds away from transforming into a blubbering idiot.

Sliding behind the wheel, Diana glanced up at the door and was taken aback when she saw Marcel still gracing the entrance. For a fleeting moment, their eyes met and those familiar butterflies took flight in the pit of her stomach. She experienced an instant recall of how his lips felt against the lobe of her ear and along the column of her neck.

What would have happened if they weren't interrupted? "I would have made love to him," was her whispered answer. She started the car and tried to block out the memory of Marcel's hands roaming up her body.

All those good feelings crashed when Marcel's very curvy friend joined him at the door. There was no mistaking that look of love and adoration that covered his features when he looked at her.

Shifting the car into gear, Diana pulled her gaze away from the smiling couple and finally left the Taylor estate.

Intermission

back at Joe Mugg's

Ophelia thanked a bright, doe-eyed waitress for refilling her coffee cup before settling her gaze back on Solomon. "I remember that day. How is it that you know so much that went on between Marcel and this Diana?"

"It took quite a bit of coaxing, trust me." Solomon chuckled into his mug.

"Still, Marcel has always been such a private person."

"True, but love has a way of changing people, I suppose." He locked onto her honey-colored gaze and a small smile flittered at the corners of his mouth.

"Maybe." She finally returned her attention to her drink. "It's just going to take me some time to get used to the idea of Casanova Brown tossing in the towel."

He took a chance and asked, "Are you disappointed?"

Ophelia frowned. "What do you mean?"

Shrugging, he tried on another smile. "I always thought you had a crush on Marcel. I remember a time back in junior high when you two were practically joined at the hip."

"Talk about hunting around in the ice age."

"He was your date for the senior prom," he added.

Her delicate arched brows lifted with surprised amusement. "It might have been because he felt sorry for me. The guy I waited to ask me out never did."

Solomon's stomach twisted into knots. "Who?"

Ophelia shook her head. "Still clueless after all this time?" She laughed. "Figures."

"You don't mean . . ." He shook his head at the preposterous thought. "Surely, you don't mean . . ."

"Yes, you," she said, leaning back in her chair and crossing her arms. "I practically made a fool of myself dropping hints and dragging you to the mall. Didn't you wonder why I wanted you to help pick out my prom dress *before* I even had a date?"

"Me?" he asked, still thunderstruck. "I thought that you were just being a . . . tease. That's why I kept picking the ugliest dresses I could find."

"Oh. I thought you were being an ass."

They laughed at the memory.

Afterward, Solomon felt silly for not catching her so-called hints. "Does this mean you liked me?"

She flashed him a sexy smile and winked. "Again, you're hunting around in the ice age."

His good mood faded when he realized what she

was saying. Whatever she'd once felt for him had long since changed. Wasn't that just his luck?

"So, tell me more about Marcel and his Cinderella."

"Funny that you should say Cinderella," Solomon said, setting his elbows on the table.

"Why?"

"Well, Uncle Willy was throwing this masquerade ball . . ."

Avoiding regret

Fifteen

one week later

After another grueling meeting with their new record distribution company, Solomon followed Marcel to his office where he quickly made himself comfortable behind the bar.

"Thank goodness that's finally over," Solomon said, reaching for his favorite bottle of vodka. "That Mr. Leonard sure knows how to drive a hard bargain."

"Tell me about it." Marcel slipped out of his jacket and loosened his tie. "He's one savvy businessman. I have to give him that much."

"But he doesn't have anything on you." Solomon lifted his glass in salute. "You're the man."

Marcel allowed the flattery to inflate his ego as he flashed his best friend a crooked smile. "I do what I can."

Solomon quickly fixed Marcel's standard rum and

Coke and brought it to his desk. "Have you decided on a costume yet?"

"Ah, the party." Marcel accepted the drink as he rolled his eyes. "I'd forgotten about it."

"Again?" Solomon took the seat in front of the desk. "You're going to try and back out of this thing, aren't you?"

"No. I'm not going to back out." He sighed because that was exactly what he wanted to do. "I said that I would go, so I'm going."

"Great." Solomon beamed. "How is your search for Mrs. Right going? Still looking to settle down with just one woman?"

Marcel nodded. "The desire is still there, though I haven't devoted too much time to pursuing it."

"Did you call that doctor I told you about?"

"I don't need a psychiatrist."

"That's what all crazy people say."

"Know many of them, do you?" Marcel laughed.

"Are you kidding? In this business they surround us. If it makes you feel any better, there are some days when I question my own sanity."

"That's no surprise. I've been questioning your sanity since junior high."

"Ha, ha." He took another sip of his drink. "Who knows, maybe you'll meet someone at the party. I told you how many women are going to be there."

"Yeah, yeah. We'll be kids in a candy shop. I remember." He shrugged, unable to generate much enthusiasm.

"You know what? I think I'm going to help you."

"What?"

Solomon set his drink down and then jumped

to his feet. "If you're serious about looking for Mrs. Taylor, then I'm going to help. And I think Uncle Willy's party is the place to hunt . . . I mean, look."

"I still don't think I follow you."

"What's not to get?" He placed his hands on Marcel's desk and leaned forward. "All the women at the ball are going to be single. Everyone will be in costumes and masks. Not only will you not know who they are, but they won't know who you are as well. So it's a perfect opportunity for you to meet a woman who doesn't know that you're the president of a record label or that you're rich as hell. It's just a man meeting a woman."

Solomon had finally piqued Marcel's interest. "Go on."

"We work the room together and whatever woman we settle on is the woman you will pursue."

The room fell silent for a long while.

"So what do you think?"

Marcel shrugged, but couldn't stop the smile from curling his lips. "It's interesting."

"So we're going to do this?"

"I might. Let me think about it some more."

"Cool." Solomon nodded and returned to his chair. "Now what's the story between you and Nora? Word around the office is that you two have more than a working relationship."

"Who's saying that?"

"Nora, I suspect." Solomon chuckled. "Lord, you were the only thing she talked about that night you deserted me in New York. Better watch your back . . . and your front with that woman around. She's determined to have you."

Marcel laughed. "It's always good to be wanted."

"Just remember your hands-off-employees policy."

Diana's soft body instantly resurfaced from his memory. He also recalled the faint scent of vanilla on her skin. "Yeah, hands-off."

Solomon frowned. "Is there something that you want to tell me?"

"Ophelia stopped by last week."

"And you're just now telling me?"

"She was just here for an afternoon. You were still in New York. No big deal."

Solomon nodded, and then after seconds passed, he asked, "Did she mention me?"

Marcel shrugged. "You might have come up once or twice."

"You're killing me. You know that?"

"Relax, man." Marcel laughed. "We just talked about old times over lunch, that's all."

Solomon visibly relaxed. "I mean, I was just wondering." He took another gulp of his drink and studied Marcel again. "Anything else you want to tell me?"

Marcel blinked and flashed his friend another awkward smile. "Nothing I can think of."

Solomon nodded, but again it didn't look like he believed him. He drained the rest of drink, his gaze locked on Marcel. "There's a speech coming, isn't there?"

Marcel swiveled to face the magnificent view of the city.

"Is it Nora?" Soloman asked.

"No."

The silence in the office grew to an unbearable decibel before Marcel faced Solomon again and stressed, "No."

Solomon sighed with relief. "Then who is it?"

"No one." Marcel stood and absently began pacing the floor. "It's nothing."

"You really should try lying to someone who doesn't know you so well," Solomon said as he stood and returned to the bar for a refill. "You asked me about Diana Guy the other day."

Marcel stopped pacing.

Solomon stopped pouring. "Oh, my God."

"Nothing's happened," Marcel started. "Well, I did kiss her."

"You kissed your secretary?"

"It was an accident."

"What, you tripped and your lips fell on hers?"

"No. I woke up and she was lying next to me."

"Whoa, whoa, whoa." Solomon set the bottle down and formed the letter T with his hands.

From the corners of his eyes, Marcel saw his office door opening.

"Time out," Solomon thundered, oblivious of the intruder.

"Mr. Taylor—"

"You slept with your secretary?"

Nora froze with her mouth gaped wide open.

Marcel clenched his jaw, tried to count to ten but got as far as five. "May I help you, Ms. Gibson?"

"I, uh, came to see if you, uh, had a chance to, uh—maybe I should come back later?" She inched back toward the door.

"Yeah, maybe you should. And while you're at it, next time ask to be buzzed in."

Nora stiffened. "I'll make sure I do that." She flashed them both a tight smile and backed out of the office. Once she was outside the door, she drew several breaths in order to regain her composure before the sound of approaching footsteps caught her attention.

"What are you doing here?" Diana asked, while shifting a stack of papers in her arms.

"I came to speak with Mar . . . Mr. Taylor about something but thought better of it."

Diana studied her for a minute and then decided she had more important things to do than to deal with whatever drama Nora might have. She returned to her desk to prioritize the documents Marcel needed to review. It took her a moment to realize that Nora hadn't budged.

"Is there something else I can help you with?" Diana asked, hardly sparing her a glance.

Nora moved toward her desk with small measured steps. "No, I was just marveling over what a sly little devil you are."

"Excuse me?"

She laughed as she waved a finger and propped a hip against Diana's desk. "That's a pretty good act you got going there, Little Miss Mouse. It's funny how I didn't catch on earlier."

Diana eased back in her chair and folded her arms. "What the hell are you talking about?"

"I'm talking about you and Marcel. Just how long have you two been an item?"

Diana laughed and rolled her eyes. "You've lost your mind."

"Have I?"

"Yes, you have." Diana rose to her feet to make it clear that she wasn't intimidated by the ambitious A&R representative. "I would also appreciate it if you could refrain from spreading such nonsense around the office."

A sinister laugh tumbled from Nora as she returned to her feet as well. "Nonsense, my ass. But let me give you fair warning. You might have him for now, but I'm a woman accustomed to getting what I want and I will have Marcel Taylor. You can bet on it."

Though she still didn't know what this crazy woman was talking about, Diana's heart squeezed painfully at the image of Nora cuddled up against Marcel. Anger and jealousy swirled within her and she could feel the extra blood rising to her head.

"What makes you think that Marcel wants you?" she hissed, not truly evaluating what she was saying.

Nora stretched out her arms. "Just look at me." She performed a perfect pirouette to show off her ample figure. "Every man wants this."

Diana's sharp retort died in her throat when Marcel's door opened and Solomon's and Marcel's hearty laughter tumbled out of the office.

"Diana, can I see you in my office?" Marcel asked once Solomon was on his way.

"Yes, sir," Diana answered but her heated gaze remained locked on Nora. "Duty calls."

"Enjoy him while you can." She gave her a departing smirk and sauntered off.

"Diana?"

"I'm coming," she barked and turned her angry gaze toward Marcel.

He held up his hands in surrender. "Whenever you're ready. I don't want to rush you or anything."

"Cut it out." She reached for her notepad and pen and stormed into Marcel's office.

Marcel closed the door behind her. "Not having a good day?"

"It's nothing I can't handle." She planted herself in the empty chair across from Marcel's desk and angrily flipped through her notepad.

The nerve of that woman. Who in the hell does she think she is?

"Diana?" Marcel frowned and leaned against the front of his desk. "Is there something wrong?"

His steady gaze was like a splash of cold water to a fire and suddenly she wasn't so sure why she let Nora, of all people, get under her skin. "I'm fine," she said, flashing her first real smile.

"Glad to hear it." He clapped his hands and straightened up. "I need a costume."

She chuckled. "Excuse me?"

He stood and returned to his desk. "It's for a masquerade ball that I don't know how to get out of. That is unless you have some ideas?"

"Fresh out." She shrugged. "Why, don't you want to go?"

"Honestly?"

"Sure, why not?"

Sighing, he eased back in his chair, but it took him a moment to compile his thoughts and in the end he just said, "It'll take too long to explain."

She stifled her disappointment, while he reached into the drawer and handed her an envelope. "Please mail this R.S.V.P. and see if you can find any costume shops around town. If you find anything, send Wayne to pick it up. He knows my sizes."

"We both do," Diana said absently as she took notes. When she realized what she'd said, she looked up.

"Yeah, I guess you do." He smiled. "And on a different note, I received a postcard from my darling mother. Seems she's now in Paris."

"Just taking a nice tour of Europe."

He nodded. "Since she's doing okay and I know where she is, you can go ahead and pull Castleman off the case. No doubt he's enjoying his free trip around the world."

"I know it's none of my business but have you heard from your father? I haven't heard from him in a week."

"No. That worries me. I've even tried to contact him myself, but he hasn't returned my calls." He sighed. "I'll swing by his place later on today and make sure that he's doing all right."

Diana nodded and jotted a note to contact Castleman. After a while, she noticed the office had fallen silent again. She looked up and caught Marcel's gaze centered on her.

Once again, the intensity of his gaze knocked her off center. "I—is there anything else?"

"I was just wondering about the other night."

Diana's body instantly turned into a carnival of activity, where her stomach hosted a family of acrobats and legions of bumper cars rammed against her heart. "What about it?"

"Well," he began. His gaze remained glued on her. "I wanted to know whether your feelings toward me have changed?"

Diana swallowed. "Changed?"

"Yeah, if I recall correctly, you weren't too fond of me. Remember?"

She forced out an awkward laugh. "Oh, that."

"Oh, that," he repeated with his own cracked laugh. "Or did my boorish behavior that next morning . . . afternoon, just cement me as the bad guy?"

"I never said you were a bad guy." She dropped her gaze to stare at a blank spot on her notepad. "I just thought you were a man with . . . too many options."

"You mean women?"

"Something like that. Even what happened between us suggests that you're a man accustomed to waking up next to women."

"Is that right?" He leaned back in his chair. "Then what was your excuse?"

The temperature in the room spiked dramatically when their gazes met again.

"If I remember correctly, you were kissing me back. Now what does that say?"

"That I was drunk out of my mind," she said defensively.

"Ah, of course." He nodded as he continued smiling. "In my defense, I thought I was dreaming."

Diana swallowed again.

"And as for my many . . . options, all it takes is the right woman to come along," he said.

"And how would you know the *right* woman?"

"I got a feeling that it'll just hit me."

Sixteen

Nora wanted to throw something. She wasn't accustomed to being beaten at anything. Especially by some plain-Jane Goody Two-shoes like Diana Guy. What on earth could Marcel Taylor see in someone like her? The woman went against the very type Nora knew he dated.

During her brief time at T&B Entertainment, Marcel had been linked at parties and in magazines with top models, singers, and actresses. Not to mention the hordes of wanna-be female musicians who were willing to do anything to sign with a major record label.

Heck, what woman wouldn't want to land him? Marcel lived life like a king. No doubt the woman who tamed him would also become music royalty.

And that was exactly what Nora had her sights set on. She needed a plan, and quick.

Stopping in the ladies' room, she struggled to devise a plan that would land the handsome executive in her bed. But the truth was she was running out of tricks to capture Marcel's attention. Whenever she'd managed to snare a private meeting, he always sidestepped her traps.

Of course, Diana didn't have that problem. She was alone with Taylor all the time. Dictation, personal errands, you name it. She was always around. Hadn't she seen her car parked outside Taylor's place just last week?

"I should have known then." She rolled her eyes. "I swear, I'm going to snatch that tired ponytail off of that girl's head." She entered a stall just as the rest room door opened.

"You should've seen Mr. Bassett in that getup," Chelsea, Solomon's secretary, said as she entered the bathroom. "He and Mr. Taylor are going to this masquerade ball. I nearly split my pants when I walked in on Solomon in a Don Juan outfit."

"Ooh, masquerade ball. Is it in New Orleans?"

Nora recognized the voice of Paula from accounting.

"Nah. His uncle is throwing it out at his place in Atlanta. So basically, it's a singles hookup. And get this, Solomon is going to try and find a *Mrs. Taylor* at the event."

Nora's ears perked up.

"You're kidding," Paula said. "Are any of the employees allowed to go to this thing?"

"You mean crash the party?" Chelsea laughed.

"Why not? I wouldn't mind hooking up with Mr. Tall, Dark, and Handsome."

"You know, you might be on to something. I saw a list of the rules and everyone is required to wear a mask and it can't be taken off until the end of the night. I imagine if you're able to win Solomon or

Marcel over by the end of the night—you're in like Flynn."

"Then let's do it. We can circulate the information to all the girls in the office. On the down low, of course. Can you get your hands on a copy of the invitation?"

"Sure," Chelsea voiced with excitement.

"Then we can have more printed and hand them out to everyone who wants to go. We can even run a pot on who will win Marcel's hand."

"This sounds fabulous," Chelsea exclaimed.

Nora smiled as she whispered, "It sure does."

Marcel pounded on his parents' door until it rattled on its hinges. What annoyed him most was that his father was home and was refusing to answer the door.

"Come on, Pop. I know you're in there." *Bang! Bang! Bang!*

Finally, it flew open and his angry father, clad in a very dirty pair of pajamas, glared at him. "You break it, you buy it," he growled and then moved away from the door.

Marcel frowned and stepped into the house. "If you'd just open the door." He followed his father from the foyer and down the hall. "How come you haven't returned my calls?"

His father grunted.

Upon entering the living room, Marcel stopped when he saw the condition of the place. "What the hell happened in here?"

"Your mother left."

Marcel's gaze roamed over the piles of clothes

on the floor. On the coffee table were dishes, potato chip bags, and peanut cans.

Donald tightened the belt on his robe. "Surely your mother and I taught you that it was rude to stare."

Marcel finally lifted his puzzled gaze up to his father. "I also remember you saying something about picking up after yourself, too." He swept his arm out to indicate the mess. "You want to tell me what's really going on here?"

"What do you care?"

Marcel noticed the red tint around his father's eyes, which meant either he'd been drinking a lot or he hadn't been sleeping. Marcel believed that it was probably a combination of both.

"Did the maid die or something?"

"I told her that her services were no longer needed. I always told your mother that there was no need to pay for something that we can do for ourselves."

"Then why aren't you doing it?"

"It's on my to-do list." Donald turned away in a huff. "What do you want, anyway? You finally found time to check on your old man?"

If Marcel knew anything, he knew neither pity nor sympathy was the way to go with his father. In fact, it was probably the quickest way to be dealt a right hook. "Actually, I realized I hadn't felt that thorn in my side in a while and I wanted to make sure that you hadn't keeled over or anything."

Donald grunted. "If your mother sent you here, then tell her I'm doing just fine without her."

"Yeah. I see that." Marcel drew a deep breath and removed his jacket. "Why don't we try to make this place a little more presentable?"

"What for? I'm not expecting anyone."

"Dad, this is unacceptable."

"This is my house. I'll do what I damn well please." He plopped down into his favorite chair and grabbed the remote.

"This doesn't look like a house. It looks more like a pigsty."

Donald didn't respond.

Pushing aside another pile of clothes on the sofa, Marcel sat down and faced his father. "I know you're a little upset that Mom left."

"Who said I was upset?"

"You don't think it's a little obvious?"

Again, Donald didn't respond.

"Look, denying what's going on here isn't going to fix the problem. Mom doesn't really want a divorce. She just wants room to be her own person. Since your retirement, you've put a lot of demands on her time."

"Since when is it a crime for a man to want to spend time with his wife?"

Marcel sighed. He might be a self-confessed connoisseur of women, but actually giving advice to his father on how to patch things up with his mother might be taking things a little too far.

"There is such a thing as smothering, Dad. That's why she's begged you to get a hobby. Mom wants to spend time with her friends, continue with her charity work at the hospital, *and* spend time with you. You, on the other hand, want her to prepare three square meals, do laundry, clean the house, and entertain you. That's unrealistic and it's not going to happen."

Donald's glare darkened. "I should've known you'd take her side. You've always been such a mama's boy."

"Ouch. You're hitting below the belt, Dad. But with all due respect, being a mama's boy has taught me how to put clothes in a washing machine and not on the sofa. I'm afraid to ask if you're wearing clean underwear."

His father grunted and returned his attention to the television.

"Dad, you can afford a maid and someone to take care of the yard. It makes no sense to live like this."

"Ha. A waste of money. Just like you and that huge place you call a house."

Oh, this is going to take some work. Marcel grabbed the remote from the arm of the chair and shut off the television. "Pop, what's really going on with you? Talk to me."

His father didn't look at him and stared at the blank screen in front of him.

Marcel eased back in his seat and crossed his legs. "Fine. I'll sit here until you start talking. We can be two funky men in a dirty house."

Donald grunted.

"Mom always said that I could be just as stubborn as you."

"She should talk," his father grumbled. "I remember one time when she forced me to sleep on the couch for a month just because I refused to eat her mother's cooking."

Marcel could sympathize. Grandma Rose tended to go a little crazy with salt. Really crazy.

Donald's shoulders slumped forward. "But I know I can be a pain."

The sudden confession surprised Marcel, but he was wise enough not to comment on the matter.

"You know," Donald continued, "I've been looking forward to retirement for as long as I can remember. Pinching pennies, cutting corners—I did everything right. The biggest risk I've ever taken was loaning you and your shadow the start-up money for T&B Entertainment."

"That investment made you a multimillionaire."

"Much to my surprise."

Marcel rolled his eyes.

Donald shook his head. "Now that I'm home, my wife doesn't want anything to do with me. She's off to God knows where, doing God knows what."

"She's in Paris. And knowing Mom like I do, she's probably wishing you were there with her. You always promised to take her around the world."

"Another waste of money."

"So what?" Marcel exclaimed. "You can afford it. It's not like you and Mom are getting any younger. These are the golden years you've been saving for. Why not enjoy them?"

"Ha. Golden years. What's so golden about them? Each day is like the day before. Your wife can't stand to be around you and your kid thinks you're nothing more than a thorn in his side." He sighed. "When I was working, at least I had something to contribute—a sense of purpose."

"Pop, you just need to learn how to relax. Have fun. Don't you know how to have fun?" As soon as he asked the question, Marcel realized that he knew the answer: no.

"You know, Pop. Maybe some of this is my fault, too. I should come around more and spend some time with you. Who knows, maybe I can teach you how to relax."

Donald laughed and held up his hand. "No offense, son. But I don't think your mother would like me hanging with you and all those women you juggle."

Marcel frowned. "There aren't that many."

His father arched an inquisitive brow.

"There might have been a couple."

Donald's other brow lifted.

"All right, all right. Whatever. It doesn't matter, because all of that is in the past. I'm looking for one woman. To have and to hold forever and ever. Just like you and Mom." He held his father's gaze. "Yeah, I know you and Mom have had your ups and downs, but I'm confident that this is just a blip in the road. You're not going to find another woman to put up with you and your idiosyncrasies. And you know it. What this situation calls for is compromises. And I'm afraid that if you don't hurry up and recognize that, you're going to lose her forever."

Donald's gaze fell to his lap before he slowly nodded in agreement. "You're right, son."

I am? Marcel breathed a sigh of relief.

"It's just that I feel so . . . worthless since I left the practice. It's like I don't have an identity anymore."

"It's just a transition, Pop. Trust me. A year from now, after spending time on a golf course . . ."

His father's sharp gaze lifted to him.

"Or fishing, or sailing—whatever you want to do, you'll realize how silly this is."

"But what if I never get used to it?"

"Then go back to work. We'll get you an office at T&B if we have to. You need to work this out with Mom."

Donald nodded, his eyes brimming with unshed

tears. "You'd think that after forty years of marriage, I'd be better equipped to handle something like this."

"Not necessarily. You've never had to deal with something like this."

"And you have?" His father laughed. "I never thought that I'd be taking advice from you."

"You don't have to say that like it's a bad thing." Marcel shifted in his seat to allow the sharp barb to roll off his shoulders.

"Yeah, you're right."

Two for two. I'm on a roll here.

After another long silence stretched between them, Donald glanced over at his son. "Were you serious about finding just one woman?"

Marcel's lips curled upward. "Afraid so."

Donald nodded again, but this time he smiled as well. "This I've got to see." He pushed himself to his feet. "I think I better hit the shower. After that, I guess I better find a travel agent. Paris, you say?"

Louisa spent her day rifling through old photo albums and diaries of a life gone by. There was a certain satisfaction in having so few regrets. She picked up a photograph of her first husband and smiled when she remembered how she had met him on her first night as a dancer. He was a horn player in the band and won her heart with his Nat King Cole–like persona.

Pain suddenly shot through Louisa's lower abdomen. She dropped the picture and doubled over. It was an eternity before the pain finally subsided and reduced her to a heaving mess on the floor. She stiffened at the sudden knock on the door.

"Ms. Louisa, are you okay in there?"

"Y-yes. I'm fine, Vicki."

A long silence stretched between her and the closed door before the nurse asked, "Would you like some lunch? I made soup and sandwiches."

"Maybe later. I was just about to take a nap." The frequent pain had stolen her appetite hours ago, not to mention she doubted she had the strength to pretend to be her normal chipper self.

"Ms. Louisa, are you sure that you're all right?"

"Just hunky-dory." Louisa grabbed hold of the bed's foot post and pulled herself up. "Give me an hour or so and then I'll join you." She drew a deep breath once she was on her feet, but suddenly she wasn't so sure that she was going to be able to walk.

Another pain stabbed her and she lost hold of the bed and tumbled to floor with a loud thud.

Vicki bolted through the door. "Ms. Louisa!"

Seventeen

Diana hated hospitals, though she couldn't imagine anyone who didn't. As she sat next to her grandmother's hospital bed and clutched her limp hands, she was reminded of another time, of another special woman: her mother.

"I'm not ready for you to leave me," she whispered, wiping away her tears. "It's too soon."

She heard the door behind her open and then close. She didn't turn to see who had entered, but knew it was Tim by the faint scent of his cologne.

"Has there been any change?" he asked.

"She opened her eyes a few minutes ago." Diana licked her dry lips. "She smiled, squeezed my hand, and then fell back to sleep."

Tim's gentle hands settled on her shoulders. "That's good news."

Diana nodded and more tears leaked from her eyes. The doctors had comforted her with talk of remission of the cancer, but she knew in her heart the time was drawing near and she would lose the last member of her family. Then what? What would she do then?

"Di, maybe you need to take a break."

"I'm fine." She shrugged his hands from her shoulders. "You can go if you like."

"I'm not leaving you or Louisa." He moved away and grabbed the chair from underneath the suspended television set.

"Does this mean that I'm going to have an audience while I'm sleeping?" Louisa's gruff voice drew their startled gasps.

"Nana." Diana squeezed her hand. "You're awake."

Louisa's eyes slowly fluttered open. "So it would seem." She glanced around. "This place again."

"When I got the call—I thought I lost you."

"*We* lost you," Tim corrected.

"Oh, you're not going to get rid of me that easily." Louisa smiled and squeezed her granddaughter's hand. "I'm not ready to leave just yet."

Diana's heart squeezed as her shoulders slumped with relief. As she stared at her frail grandmother, a list of what-ifs filled her head.

"No need to worry about things that are out of our control," Louisa said as if reading Diana's mind.

"But is it something we can't control? What if through the treatments you could beat this thing?"

"And what if I can't?"

"Then at least I know I've done everything to prevent . . ." She sighed. "Giving up will always leave a door of questions open."

Louisa's smile grew wider as her gaze became more loving. "Baby, I'm not going to live forever. This is a question of quality, not quantity. I'm probably not going to make it through the next three years. I know and understand. Now it's time that you do, too."

Diana shook her head, not wanting to accept her Nana's words.

"Denial is only going to cause you more pain."

Tim stood from his chair. "I'll give you two some time alone."

The two women said nothing as they waited for him to leave the room.

"I'm not in denial." Diana closed her eyes but realized she wasn't being honest. "Okay . . . maybe just a little. Three years?"

"Could be less, could be more."

Louisa licked her lips and Diana quickly reached for the pitcher of water by the bed. She then helped Louisa sip from a plastic cup and repositioned her for added comfort.

"Thanks," Louisa said, her smile ever present.

Diana shook her head, not sure how her grandmother could take such a serious matter so lightly.

"Baby girl," Louisa said, reaching for her hand again. "It's time for you to live. That's what I intend on doing for whatever time I have left. I've had a fun and full life. I'm now looking forward to seeing what this heaven place is all about. I want to see my beautiful daughter again. Not to mention I have two handsome husbands waiting as well." She winked.

Diana couldn't help laughing. "You're something else."

"True. But I'm still worried about you, sweetie."

"Why on earth would you be worried about me?"

Louisa sighed as she thought over her next words. "I'm worried because you won't live. Life is happening right now all around you and you don't know what to do with it. Travel; see the world. Trust yourself; discover yourself. Find love; give love. Do whatever it takes to be happy. Only then at the end of your own journey can you lie in a hospital bed with no regrets and looking forward to the next adventure."

Diana allowed her grandmother's words to penetrate her heart and even felt them inspire her imagination. Why couldn't she travel the world or discover all the different sides of herself? As for love—wasn't she already in love? But was he a person worthy of real love or just a good time?

After placing his father on a plane for France, Marcel returned to his parents' house and promptly called a reputable maid service to perform a miracle. He weighed whether he should call and warn his mother that Donald was on his way, but in the end decided to let his father surprise her.

He didn't know what he would do if, in fact, his instincts were wrong and his mother truly wanted to be alone. But he knew for sure that if she returned to her house in the condition he'd found it, the chances of a divorce would undoubtedly multiply.

It was nearly two in the morning when the maid service completed the job and Marcel wrote a check for double the amount of the invoice. They deserved it.

Too tired to drive home, Marcel retired to his old bedroom. It amazed him how his mother still refused to change the room, but it pleased him as well. He lay down on the water bed he'd convinced his parents to buy back in the early eighties, knowing that in the morning his back might be a little stiff. But for this moment of nostalgia, he was willing to take that chance.

His gaze darted around the room and the various posters. Happy memories floated in his head as he stared at the likes of Dr. J and Magic Johnson. When he saw Larry Bird smiling back at him, he remembered the grief he got from the other kids on the block. The same was when he put up posters of Pete Rose and Joe Montana.

All in all, Marcel had had a wonderful childhood and so far a pretty good adult life. But there was still that hole. That very large hole in his life.

He thought over the deal he'd made with Solomon and now wondered whether it was a wise or even logical thing to do.

Probably not.

What qualities should he look for in a wife? A good cook—certainly. Someone warm, nice, and understanding. A sense of humor would be good. Oh, she must like animals. He thought about Diana and how he'd found her in the bottom of a closet and he couldn't help laughing out loud.

He'd known people who were afraid of dogs, but she took the cake. However, whenever he was around her, he was . . . comfortable. He frowned as he thought it over, but then shrugged it off.

There had to be plenty of women he was comfortable around. Ophelia was a good example. His thoughts went silent as he tried to come up with another name. Well, there was always Mom, he realized, but then laughed at himself when he heard his father's voice calling him a mama's boy.

"Diana," he whispered. "Di." Her image instantly materialized in his mind. And like always he smiled at her perfections as well as her imperfections. In addition to her slightly off-centered nose, he'd discovered that one breast was slightly fuller than the other.

Marcel shook his head. This was definitely something a boss shouldn't know about his secretary. His thoughts lingered on the afternoon he'd wakened next to her. More importantly, he remembered the kiss they shared. There was so much passion behind it. He could honestly say that he'd never felt anything quite like it before.

"One lover," he said into the dark. That was also different, considering this day and age. "And her first time was in college."

Hell, he barely remembered his first time. He was sixteen, maybe fifteen. And even then it was with an older woman. Rachel Johnson was eighteen with dimples like Janet Jackson's. During the week after he'd lost his virginity, he was convinced that he was in love. He'd even bragged about it to all his friends.

That was until he and half the high school football team witnessed Rachel necking with some college jock at the Varsity.

So much for love.

But now after so much time had passed, love was the very thing he craved.

Sighing, Marcel found his eyes growing heavy and proving difficult to keep open. As sleep descended, Diana's soft features remained in focus while he wondered fleetingly whether she was a good cook.

* * *

Diana fumbled her way into her apartment at God knows what time. The fact that she had to be at work in a few hours was laughable at best. If it hadn't been for Louisa's insistence that she go home, Diana would still be curled up in the reclining chair next to Louisa's hospital bed.

It was a good thing Tim had accompanied her. She could barely walk, let alone drive. She locked the front door and then soaked up the silence of the apartment. This would be what it would sound like when her grandmother . . .

Drawing a deep breath, Diana tried to shake the thought from her head, but it wouldn't go away.

She pushed open her bedroom door, but didn't go inside. The light in her grandmother's room drew her attention and instead she headed in that direction.

At the door's entrance, she smiled at the incredibly feminine décor. Golden floral prints intermingled with old Chantilly lace and there was even the weird combination of rose water and BenGay wafting in the air. The room brought a sad smile to her lips.

When her eyes fell to the trunk at the foot of the bed, she grew curious at the clutter around it. She walked over and sat down among the letters and photographs. She was familiar with most of them, but there were a few that raised her eyebrows.

"Yeah, right. Burlesque." Diana smiled. As she shuffled through the old pictures, she wondered why her grandmother never pursued an acting career. Judging by the pictures, Louisa Mae Styles could have given Dorothy Dandridge a run for her money.

In pictures Diana witnessed Louisa's first African safari, the thrill of her first flying lesson, and the first time she attempted to climb Mt. Everest. Key word there was *attempted*.

Then came the pictures of two weddings. Of course she was beautiful in both of them. Not to mention that she had snagged two very attractive, yet different men. The first husband was a professional musician who died before his time in a tour bus accident. The second husband, the one Diana knew as Grandpa, died from a massive heart attack around the time of the Iran Contra hearings.

One thing for sure, Louisa was right. She'd lived a full life and had apparently enjoyed every moment of it.

Exhaustion finally embraced Diana. She climbed up from the floor and dove into Louisa's bed as a matter of convenience. The photograph remained prominent in her mind as she fantasized by replacing the men in Louisa's life with images of Marcel Taylor.

The cut-and-paste images in her mind showed the couple they would make on their wedding day. In truth, they made quite a couple. A beautiful couple. "Find love and give love." Louisa's voice drifted around her. Maybe it was time that Diana did just that.

Eighteen

It was not the day to be late for work, Marcel realized moments after he'd arrived. He'd missed his meeting with DreamWorks regarding producing future soundtracks. After that, he had scheduled interviews with *Vibe* and *The Source* magazines.

But what bothered him most now was Diana's absence.

"You know, you could call someone when you're planning to bail out on a meeting," Solomon said, following Marcel into his office.

"My bad, man." Marcel said, settling behind his desk. "You wouldn't believe the day I had yesterday with Pop."

Solomon held up his hands. "Say no more."

Marcel laughed, but still didn't divulge what his parents were going through at the moment. Maybe after everything was resolved he would talk about it. "You haven't heard from Diana this morning, have you?"

"Not a word. I was actually starting to think you two were together somewhere."

Marcel frowned as he looked up at him.

Solomon just shrugged. "Hey, you're the one with the runaway lips."

"That's not funny."

"It wasn't meant to be." He winked and slid his hands into his pants pockets. "Maybe I should invite Diana to the masquerade ball so she could be a contender in our little project."

"You're a regular comedian this morning."

"You mean this afternoon." Solomon eased into the chair across from Marcel. "It was just a thought. After all, you kissed her because you thought it was a dream. I don't know, I might be out in left field, but maybe your subconscious is trying to tell you something."

A snappy reply eluded Marcel.

A wide grin split Solomon's face as if he read something in his friend's expression. "There's something you're not telling me."

Diana meant to grab just a few hours of sleep before returning to the hospital, but instead woke up well into the afternoon.

"Oh, my God." She scrambled out of bed and tripped onto the floor.

"Diana?" Tim's voice drifted down the hall, and in the next second the door to Louisa's bedroom jerked open.

She blinked as she stared up at him. "What are you doing here?" she asked, standing.

"Lou and I just arrived a half hour ago."

"Nana?" Diana pushed past him and rushed to the living room where, sure enough, Lou sat in her favorite spot on the sofa. "What are you doing here?"

"I live here, silly."

Tim joined them as he leaned against the antique upright piano. "She insisted on being released this morning."

"I tried to call you," Louisa said and took a sip of her tea. "But apparently you didn't hear the phone."

"Yeah, when we got here you were sleeping like a log."

Diana remained confused. "Did the doctor say it was all right for you to leave?"

"Doctors don't know everything," Louisa snorted and then flashed a wide smile. "According to them I should have kicked the bucket years ago."

Diana held her tongue and thought better of giving a speech or lecture. What difference would it make? Louisa Mae was going to do what she wanted. She always had. So instead, Diana walked over to her and leaned down to give her a long, tight hug. "Sorry, I didn't hear the phone."

Louisa affectionately patted her arm. "Don't worry about it. Apparently, you needed the rest."

Tim moved from the wall to a recliner. "Frankly, I thought your workaholic butt went to work."

"Work!" Diana jumped with wide eyes. "Ohmigosh." She raced over to the phone, but hesitated before picking it up.

"What is it, dear?" Louisa asked, frowning.

"Maybe I should go in and explain what happened. It's sort of late to be calling, don't you think?"

Tim looked at his watch. "It's just after one. Given the circumstances, I think he'll understand."

"Yeah." Diana bobbed her head. "You're right." She picked up the phone, but then put it down again. "I still think maybe I should go in and talk to him."

Tim chuckled. "You can't miss work for one day, can you?"

"I'm not going in to actually work. I think I should talk to Marcel . . . Mr. Taylor." She nodded. "You know, I think I'm going to take a few days . . . a week . . . a couple of weeks off to spend with Nana."

Tim's and Lou's brows rose in surprise.

Diana lifted her chin, once again feeling Louisa's words from last night inspire her. "And when I get back, we're all going out to dinner. That's if you're up to it."

Louisa clapped her hands together. "I'm always up for a night out."

Diana smiled. "I think we can manage it." She turned and went to get ready.

Given the late hour, Marcel grew concerned over Diana's absence. Had she told him that she would be off today?

"She must have," he answered himself, but still debated whether he should place a call to her home or cell phone to make sure.

He left his office and went out to Diana's desk to see if anything was written on her day calendar. When he sat behind her desk, he was disappointed to find no notation on the day's date about being out. However, there was something sticking out from beneath the calendar.

Marcel pulled out a sheet of paper and turned it over to see that it was a letter addressed to him.

"Letter of resignation?" He looked up to see if anyone was in the vicinity and then quickly folded the paper and stuffed it into his jacket.

"Mr. Taylor?"

His heart leaped as his eyes jumped up to a frowning Diana.

"What are you doing at my desk?"

He blinked, momentarily stumped as to why he was out there himself.

Her brows lifted. "Are you looking for something?"

"Y-yes." He stood. "I came to take a look at your calendar to see if you'd marked a doctor's appointment or something." He forced an awkward smile. "I didn't remember you telling me that you'd be off today."

She nodded as if satisfied with his answer. "No, I didn't. Do you mind if we go into your office? I want to talk to you about that."

Marcel's heart squeezed. Was she about to resign now? "Sure." He smiled again and then led the way to his office. He held the door open as she entered and pretended the sweet smell of vanilla that clung to her skin had no effect on him.

"So," he said, closing the door. "What can I do for you?" *Please, don't quit.*

Diana clasped her hands in front of her. "I need to take some time off."

The air in Marcel's chest rushed from his lungs as his shoulders slumped in relief. "Time off?" *Thank God.*

"I know this is on short notice but . . . the truth

is my grandmother is sick. And I want to spend some time with her."

Whatever he had expected her to say, it wasn't this. "I'm sorry to hear that." He quickly remembered the feisty little old lady from Club Secrets and he was surprised that she was actually sick. "Is there anything I can do?"

"No. I just need to take this time off."

He nodded. "Of course. Take as long as you need."

"I can call that temporary service we always use for a replacement."

"Don't worry about that. I'll get someone in human resources to take care of it." He paused, and then asked the question he really wanted to know. "Do you know how much time you'll need?"

She dropped her gaze. "I'm not really sure. A few weeks, maybe a month."

Again he nodded. "Why don't we say six weeks for now and then you can call and let me know if you need more?"

"I doubt I can afford that much time off," she said disappointedly.

"You have plenty of vacation time, plus you've never used any of your sick time either. So I'm sure that you have more than enough to cover it."

Her smile seemed more relaxed as she looked up at him. "You're probably right."

When their gazes locked, the room filled with silence while the temperature climbed a few degrees.

"You *are* coming back, right?" he asked.

"I plan to. Yes."

"Good." He smiled, but doubt lingered in his

mind. He did after all have her letter of resignation burning a hole in his pocket.

"Well, I guess I better get going," she said, stepping backward. "Thanks so much for understanding on such short notice."

"Not a problem."

She turned away, but he stopped her when her hand landed on the doorknob.

"We're going to miss you around here."

The loud silence returned before Diana glanced over her shoulder at him. "I'll miss you guys, too." She opened the door and waltzed out.

When it closed behind her, she drew in a deep breath and released it in a long sigh. Even still her heart continued to race. Once again, she'd imagined Marcel meant more than what was said. She was also sure that she misread his dark searching gaze when she stood before him.

"You and your wishful thinking."

"There you are, Diana." Chelsea rushed over to her. "I was wondering where you were today."

"Oh, hey, Chelsea." Diana moved over to her desk to take a few things home. "What can I do for you?"

"Actually." Chelsea lowered her voice as she followed her. "It's more like what I can do for you."

Diana frowned. "What do you mean?"

"Well, surely you heard about the masquerade ball that Mr. Taylor and Mr. Bassett are going to next week?"

"Oh, you mean the one Mr. Taylor doesn't want to go to?"

Chelsea giggled. "That's probably it. Well, this is the ball all the girls are dying to attend."

"The girls in the office?"

"Yep."

Diana shrugged. "Why?"

Chelsea emitted another giggle and then leaned in closer. "Because this is the place where Marcel Taylor is going to search for his future wife."

Nineteen

Diana stared at the dummy invitation to William Bassett's masquerade ball while Chelsea explained the crazy idea she and Paula had cooked up. The whole thing sounded ridiculous. No way Marcel would take such a serious decision lightly—let alone allow his best friend to arbitrarily select his future wife.

"So are you going to attend?" Chelsea asked. "It should be a lot of fun."

Diana shook her head. "I doubt it." She handed back the invitation. "I'm not particularly interested in becoming Mrs. Marcel Taylor."

"Then you're an exception." Chelsea snickered. "What's not to want? He's gorgeous, rich, wonderful, and rich. I'd die if he selected me."

Diana just laughed. "What's stopping him from selecting you now?"

"Oh, don't spoil it for us with logic. This is supposed to be fun." Chelsea pushed the invitation back into her hands and then winked. "Think it over. We all owe it to ourselves to have a little fun in life."

Propped against a mound of pillows, Louisa delighted herself with the sheer entertainment Tim provided. Decked out in fuschia boas and the best wig Star Jones provided, he belted out a special rendition of the disco hit "I Will Survive."

"Fabulous!" She clapped exuberantly. "You should be in show business."

"You really think so?" Tim plopped down on the end of her bed. "There was a time when I used to wow the crowds at this cool club in South Miami Beach." He leaned forward. "That's how I really met Caleb, you know."

"Ah." She rolled her eyes back and instantly recalled the thrill of dancing before a crowd. "There's nothing like performing in front of an audience, is there?"

"I bet you were great."

Louisa nodded. "Yes, I was."

The sound of the apartment's front door closing drew their attention.

"Diana, is that you?"

"Yeah, it's me," Diana answered and followed the sound of her grandmother's voice to her bedroom. The minute she pushed open the door and saw Tim in his getup, her eyes widened and laughter burst from her lungs.

Tim timidly reached up and removed the wig.

"Sorry. I'm sorry," she said, shaking her head. "I just wasn't expecting—"

He held up his hand. "No need to apologize. I'm sure it was a shock."

"Oh, Diana. You should have seen him," Louisa said, pushing herself up. "He's great." She glanced at Tim. "Go on. Show her."

Embarrassed, Tim waved her off.

Diana sensed that she'd inadvertently hurt Tim's feelings and crossed over to sit on the bed as well. "Yeah, what is it? I'd like to see it."

"It's nothing," Tim insisted.

"It's wonderful," Louisa encouraged.

Diana brightened. "Then let me see it."

Tim hesitated a moment longer and then quickly grabbed the wig and repositioned it on his head.

Diana's mood lightened when Tim jumped up and wrapped the boa around his neck. But nothing could prepare her for when he pressed the play button on his portable stereo. A few minutes later when he ended his performance, she applauded and bound off the bed to embrace him.

"That was great. I didn't know you were a performer."

"Well, it's about the only thing I keep in the closet nowadays." He laughed.

"I think that you need to find a stage," Louisa said.

"Nah," he said. "It's just something that I like to do in the mirror when I should be vacuuming."

"Liar," Louisa and Diana said in unison and then laughed at themselves.

"Looks like I should give you the same speech I gave Diana about taking risks," Louisa said, waving a pointed finger. "You're never going to get anywhere by keeping your dreams to yourself."

"Really?" Tim looked over at Diana. "And what exactly is your dream?"

As she felt both sets of eyes centered on her,

Diana's throat squeezed shut. "Nothing. I don't have one."

Tim frowned. "Cut it out. We all have dreams or some deep, dark secret that we're afraid to admit even to ourselves."

Diana shrugged as she delivered the lie without thinking. "Not me."

"Someone is in denial," Louisa singsonged.

Diana's mouth opened prepared to protest again, but the invitation in her purse crossed her mind.

"Jed, I think we've struck oil," Louisa gushed.

Sucking in her bottom lip, Diana felt her belly swarm with butterflies. "A dark secret that we're afraid to admit to ourselves?"

"Yes?" Tim and Louisa looked at her with hopeful eyes.

Louisa stood from the bed and both she and Tim crowded around Diana.

Then as if realizing what she was about to do, she shook her head and waved the notion off. "Oh, never mind."

"No, no," they said. "Go on."

Diana hesitated.

"Remember what I said about regret," Louisa said. "A life full of regret is no life at all."

Diana sat back on the bed and contemplated what she wanted to say. "There's this guy," she began.

Like an avalanche, Tim and Louisa dropped onto the bed next to her, their attention rapt on what she was about to say next.

It was hard to choose her words mainly because it was the first time she had spoken them out loud. "It's not that I actually stand a chance with him or anything. If fact, as a woman, I don't think he even notices me. Except for that time we kissed."

"What?" Tim and Louisa chimed.

"What do you mean as a woman, dear?" Louisa added. "How else is he supposed to know you?"

"And when did this kiss take place?" Tim wanted to know.

How much more should she tell them? she wondered. What if they laughed at her? Once again the invitation floated to the forefront of her mind.

"Because he only sees me as his dutiful secretary," Diana said, but it came out as a low whisper. When she looked around, she noticed both had leaned in close to catch her words. Then she saw the slow dawning in their eyes.

Squealing, they grabbed her into a bear hug.

Being pulled in two different directions, Diana fleetingly thought that they were going to snap her in half.

"Guys, do you mind? You're hurting me."

"I knew it. I knew it," Louisa said, pulling away and then wiping her tears of joy.

"Marcel Taylor." Tim sobbed. "*The* Marcel Taylor. I knew it when I picked you up that day." He kissed her cheek.

Diana frowned as she leaned back. "Ugh. Your wig is tickling me."

"Sorry." He snatched it off of his head and grabbed her again.

"Hold up." Diana pulled away. "It's not like I've won him over or anything."

"Yet!" Tim and Louisa said and then looked at each other.

"Great minds think alike," Louisa said.

"I don't know about that," Diana said. "A part of me thinks I should get my head examined." She stood from the bed. "Mr. Taylor isn't the kind of man to settle down with just one woman. I should know. I've sent plenty of flowers and gifts to his legions of women over the past two years. I'm not looking to settle for a man that's considered community property."

"Surely he's not that bad," Louisa said, but then blinked when Tim and Diana gave her an *oh, yes, he is* look.

"Okay, then. Who said anything about settling? How come you just can't date him, change him, and then marry him?"

Diana rolled her eyes. "Nana, that's irrational. No one should go into a relationship with the mind-set of trying to change someone."

"Why not? Women have been doing it since the days of Adam."

"People have to want to change. It's not something that you force on them."

"Oh, pooh. We're talking about men. They don't know what they want. Nor do they know what's good for them. The art is changing a man without him knowing you're changing him."

"Amen," Tim atoned.

Diana waved off their reasoning. "Marcel has probably been subjected to every trick in the book by now and by women more skilled than I. Besides, I don't want a man that I have to trick into liking or falling in love with me."

Louisa looked to Tim. "Do you hear what I hear?"

"I hear a symphony," Tim sang.

Diana stood and rolled her eyes. "I'm not going to talk to you guys if you're not going to be serious about this."

"Okay. We're sorry," Tim said.

"Yeah, we're sorry." Louisa stared up at her. "So you hate my idea. What are you going to do?"

Diana blinked. "Do? I'm not going to *do* anything. I like the guy. That's it."

Tim and Louisa glanced at each other.

"Though he might be looking for a wife," Diana added.

Her grandmother and best friend exploded with new questions.

"I thought you said that he wasn't looking to settle down?" Louisa asked.

"How come he can't marry you?"

"It's just a rumor," Diana said, shrugging.

"Any chance there's some truth to it?" Louisa asked.

"I doubt it." Diana hugged herself as she thought it over. "Then again . . ."

Louisa stood with a wide smile and looped her arm around Diana's waist. "Then that settles it. You have to at least try to win his heart. Who knows? Maybe he really is ready to settle down. All playboys retire after a while and some go on to make terrific husbands. Not all, but some. And I have to tell you, I got a good vibe off of him a few weeks ago. He definitely has potential."

Diana rolled her eyes again. "We're talking like I actually have a chance with this man. Let me tell you, I don't. He dates women with booties like J. Lo and Beyoncé. Women who were born perfect." Her thoughts centered on Ophelia.

"What are you talking about? You're very pretty." Louisa squeezed her. "Any man would be lucky to have you."

"Yeah." Tim also draped an arm around her. "Now tell us about this kiss."

"Oh, that."

"Yeah, that," Tim and Louisa said.

Diana took a deep breath and explained what had happened the night she stayed at Marcel's. When she was done, she swore she could have heard a pin drop in Texas.

"Well, someone say something."

Louisa cleared her throat. "So, you mean if this Nora person didn't show up—"

"I didn't say that."

"You didn't have to," Tim said. "Wow. You have more skills than you're letting on."

The invitation returned to her memory once again and she spoke without censoring her words. "There's this masquerade ball coming up next week. I was told that he might be looking for . . . a possible wife at the event."

"That settles it," Tim said. "You have to go."

"Me and all the single women at the office. They're all going to crash the party as well. But it's ridiculous. If Marcel wanted to date one of us, there's nothing stopping him. He has a rule about dating women he works with . . . though I do see him with Nora a lot."

"Then don't let him know it's you," Louisa said simply.

"Of course he's going to know it's me. I work with the man six days a week."

Tim removed the boa from around his neck. "You just need a good disguise."

"A new hairstyle," Louisa suggested. "Maybe a good wig."

"Color contact lenses," Tim added.

"Oh, a tight, revealing outfit."

"Oh, please. The minute he's in front of me, he's going to recognize me," Diana reasoned.

Louisa snapped her fingers. "Then you'll also need an elaborate mask. It is a masquerade party, after all."

"What do you suggest I do when I open my mouth? I still sound like me."

That threw them for a loop for a moment, but then Tim snapped his fingers. "French. Wasn't French your minor in college?"

Diana shrugged. "Yeah."

"Then you'll speak French the entire evening. That'll add a mysterious aura about you. Every time you speak I want you to be very breathy with it. Be very dramatic, that ought to alter your voice a little."

"And we need to teach you a new way to walk," Louisa said. "I can teach you how to work those hips. The magic is in the hips." She and Tim high-fived each other.

Diana's heart fluttered with excitement as she too began to picture what they had in mind. But could it work? "I don't know, guys."

"All right. Enough of this," Louisa said. "You need to make a decision. Do you want him or not?"

Diana returned to the edge of the bed. "But even if I did—"

"I didn't ask you that. Do you want him or not? No hedging or offering excuses."

Diana gulped.

"Yes or no?" her grandmother pressed.

It was the moment of truth, Diana realized. Not

because she was confessing to her grandmother and her best friend, but because she was admitting it to herself as well.

Tim and Louisa waited.

Diana drew a deep breath just as she felt her eyes glaze over. "I want him with all my heart."

Another intermission

back at Joe Mugg's

"When the hell are we getting to this masquerade ball?" Ophelia asked, glancing at her watch. "I'll be eligible for Medicare benefits by the time you finish this story."

Solomon frowned. "You're the one who asked for it, remember?"

"Yeah, but most people tell a story in a couple of minutes, not during the entire course of a presidential term. When are you going to get to the juicy stuff?"

"Patience. I'm getting there." He smiled. "Or maybe I should stop and let Marcel tell you the rest?"

"I swear to goodness if you leave me hanging, you're limping out of here."

"Well, I might be persuaded to finish if you tell me a little more about that prom you wanted me to take you to."

Ophelia's shoulders slumped. "There's nothing else to tell. I wanted you to take me, you didn't ask, so *c'est la vie*. Then, of course, there was also the senior prom but hey."

Solomon stared at her. "I don't believe this. Why are we just now talking about this? I wanted to take you to both of those, but I thought that you had a thing for Marcel. God knows you were always around him."

"I was always around both of you." She shrugged. "I thought I was giving you plenty of hints on how I felt, but you just ignored them, or so I thought."

"Did Marcel know?" He thought of his best buddy and couldn't imagine that he would keep something this vital from him especially since Marcel knew of his feeling toward Ophelia.

"I never came out and said it, but I suspect that he knew."

"And you and Marcel . . . ?"

"Please. Marcel is like a big brother to me. But you . . . I don't know. I liked you the first time I tackled you in touch football when I was ten years old."

Solomon swallowed. "You don't say."

"I do say." She smiled. "Now, back to this story."

He blinked, but shook his head. "I have to ask another question about us first."

Ophelia's lips drooped as her gaze locked on her coffee cup.

Solomon felt his throat constrict to the point that he could barely get air through, let alone words. "How do you feel about me now?"

She closed her eyes for so long, he thought she wasn't going to respond.

"Never mind. You don't have to answer that right now," he rushed to say, fearful of her answer.

"I still care for you very much," she finally said. "I've just come to accept that we weren't meant to be. We're where we're supposed to be: friends."

Solomon stared into her honey-colored eyes and felt himself nod though he didn't want to. "Yeah. It's probably best."

There was an awkward silence as the two sipped their coffee.

Solomon was first to recover. Mainly because he was determined not to ruin the rest of the afternoon. Maybe some things were best left in the past. "So, where was I in the story?"

Ophelia cleared her throat and then flashed him a shaky smile. "Uh, I believe this Diana had just enlisted her burlesque dancing grandma and her ambitious, gay, cross-dressing best friend to help her transform herself for this mysterious masquerade ball."

"Oh, yes. I remember now. . . ."

A heart can't
be fooled

Twenty

On the night of Uncle Willy's masquerade ball, Marcel gave serious thought to backing out of the gig. Especially since Solomon was taking this "find a wife" thing so seriously. It was funny that a man who was afraid to approach the woman of his dreams was actually trying to help him find a wife.

He stared back at his reflection in the mirror and adjusted his tie. Of course, he had no intention of actually marrying just anyone. He would go out with whomever his buddy selected. No harm in seeing if there was a connection. People have met their soul mates under stranger conditions.

"Are you nervous?" Solomon asked, entering Marcel's bedroom in a tux.

Marcel smiled. "You still bummed that this isn't a costume party?"

"Yeah. Who knew there was a difference between a masquerade costume party and a ball?"

"Well, I'm glad. Did you see the costume that Diana and Wayne picked out for me?" He retrieved a bright red satin costume and a pitchfork from the closet.

"The devil?" Solomon asked with a broad grin.

"Yep. Complete with a cape and pitchfork." He tossed the ensemble onto the bed. "You think she was trying to tell me something?"

"It depends. Was she due for a raise?" Solomon laughed.

"I don't know. Maybe I should check into it."

"Or"—Solomon's voice rose—"maybe she's getting you back for your lips falling onto hers a few weeks ago."

Marcel gave him a stern look.

"What? Anything is possible."

"That's not funny."

"Again, it wasn't meant to be." Solomon slid his hands into his pockets and then rocked on his feet. "How long has she been out of the office now?"

"A week."

"And you haven't hired a temp yet?"

Marcel didn't say anything. How would he explain that he didn't want to see someone else sitting behind Diana's desk without it becoming a big deal? Hell, he wasn't quite sure if he understood it either.

"Okay. I take it you don't want to talk about it."

"There's nothing really to talk about. I just haven't gotten around to . . . to . . ."

"Replacing her," Solomon finished for him.

"Yeah." Marcel was careful to avoid his friend's gaze as he reached over and picked up his black mask with tiny speckles of gold around the eyes and shook his head. "I feel like we're going trick-or-treating."

"Ah, stop being a baby and put it on. The sooner

we get there, the sooner we can get the whole thing over with."

"I think I'll wait until we get there." He took a final glance in the mirror, but then made no move to leave for the party. Instead his thoughts fluttered in a cloud of depression, one he hadn't been able to shake for a solid week.

"Hey, man. What's troubling you?"

"Nothing." He waltzed away from the mirror and headed out of his bedroom. "Are you ready to go?"

Brandy popped up from her dog bed in the corner of the room and followed the men down the long hallway to the staircase.

"This policy of yours about dating employees—"

"Don't even go there," Marcel said without breaking his stride.

"I'm just saying that it's not like it's against the law or anything."

"Thanks for the news flash."

Woof!

"Not you too." Marcel rolled his eyes.

Solomon laughed. "Hey, we both can't be wrong."

Marcel removed his keys from the foyer table and turned back toward Solomon. "Even if I wanted to date Diana, which I'm not saying I do, it would never happen. The woman doesn't like me."

"What makes you say that?"

"She told me. I'm an insatiable playboy and a driven workaholic who's stingy when it comes to raises."

"Wow. She said that?"

"I believe those were her exact words." He crossed his arms and leaned against the door. "In the office she goes out of her way to avoid eye contact and a lot of times I feel as if she's dying to get away from me. You should have seen her the night I took her and her grandmother home from Club Secrets. You would have thought that I'd slashed her tires or something."

"You didn't, did you?"

"Of course I didn't," Marcel huffed. "I'm just not the kind of guy she likes to date."

Solomon also crossed his arms, while curiosity twisted his expression. "And what exactly is her type?"

"Monogamous politicians."

"Is there such a thing?"

Marcel shrugged. "It was news to me, too."

After four hours of preparations, Diana didn't recognize the woman staring back at her in the vanity mirror. Her once black hair had been lightened to a warm chestnut with honey highlights. Then Tim created a masterpiece by adding extensions for an eighties big-hair look.

With contacts, she transformed her brown eyes to a convincing hazel green. But none of that compared to the dramatic makeup Louisa applied to her face, complete with a set of false eyelashes.

"It's beautiful," Diana whispered in awe.

"No." Louisa pressed her face next to Diana's. "You're the one who's beautiful. You're going to knock his socks off tonight."

Diana's heart dropped as her eyes widened with what she was about to do.

Louisa gave her an affectionate squeeze. "Don't worry. You can do this."

"I can do this," Diana reaffirmed.

Tim grabbed a tissue from the vanity table and

wiped his eyes. "I wish Caleb could see you. This is a Kodak moment. Does anyone have a camera?"

Louisa straightened. "There's one on top of the dresser. Do you mind?"

Tim rushed across the room and found the camera.

"Well, let me get into the dress first. I don't want you taking pictures of me in my underwear." Diana popped up and went to get her dress when Louisa stopped her.

"Ah, ah, ah. That's not how I taught you to walk."

Contrite, Diana slowed her stride and gave her hips a slight rotation as she continued toward the bed for her dress.

"That's better," Louisa praised. "Oh, you're going to be fabulous. I wish I could go."

"I'd settle for being a fly on the wall," Tim chimed in.

Diana wondered if it was too late to back out of the plan.

"What time is Charlie's cousin coming with the limousine?" Tim asked.

Diana glanced at her watch. "He should be here at eight o'clock. I have to make sure I get something for Charlie for helping out like this."

"Everyone wants to make this a special night for you, dear. You deserve it."

"I don't know about that." Diana's mouth curled into a half smile. "Right now, I'm just hoping I don't embarrass myself, but I probably shouldn't get my hopes up."

Louisa waved off her concerns. "You're going to do fine."

Diana stared down at her dress for the evening.

It had been an old dress from her grandmother's *entertainment* days, updated with a modern flare from Tim.

Diana had no doubts that she would garner some attention in the dress. She just hoped it would be the right kind.

"Oh, just get on with it." Tim rushed over to her and set the camera down. "I'll help you."

A few minutes later, Diana twirled around in front of her audience. "So, what do you think?"

Louisa clapped her hands together, and then pressed them against her closed lips as her eyes shimmered with joy. "Perfect."

"Just remember you have to be out of there by midnight because Jimmy has to return the limo before his boss realizes it's gone."

"Got it."

Tim snapped a picture and replied, "It's time for you to show Marcel Taylor just what he's been missing."

William Bassett made his millions in real estate. Though it was true that he was no Donald Trump, that didn't stop him from living and enjoying a life of excess. His thirty-thousand-square-foot home nestled between Atlanta and Roswell was one of his most prized possessions.

Marcel's limousine rolled down the long driveway, while he prepared to deal with Uncle Willy's over-the-top personality.

"What happened to the old Casanova Brown? Just relax and try to have a good time," Solomon said, winking. "I'll hook you up with a winner."

Marcel smiled and slid on his mask just as their

vehicle slowed to a stop. It was too late to turn around now. He might as well go with the flow.

Charlie opened the back door and Marcel stepped out into the night's cool breeze and was amazed at the turnout. Yes, Willy Bassett had friends, but it looked as though the man had invited half the state to the event.

"It looks like I'm going to have my job cut out for me tonight," Solomon whispered, appearing beside Marcel.

"That would be an understatement." He looked at his friend and tried not to laugh at what looked like a sleeping mask with the eyes cut out.

"Hey, it looked better with my Don Juan costume." Solomon shrugged.

"Sure it did."

Together they strolled up to the open oak doors where both reached inside their jackets to present their invitations.

"Have a good evening, gentlemen," the man stationed at the door said and then gestured them inside.

Marcel moved into the gold marble foyer and his eyes immediately widened at the sight of beautiful bodies adorned in glittering gowns. He had to admit that everyone being in a mask did add a dash of mystery.

"You know," he said over his shoulder to Solomon. "I just might be able to get into this after all."

"That's good news."

"Ah, boys." Willy's boisterous voice sliced through the ballroom music seconds before he squeezed his rotund shape in between the two men. "I wondered what time you two would get here." His heavy arms crashed on each of their shoulders.

"We wouldn't have missed it for the world," Solomon assured him. "But how did you recognize us?"

"Are you kidding?" Willy thundered and playfully popped Solomon on the back of the head. "I would know my only nephew with blindfolds on."

Marcel rolled his eyes and smiled at the exaggeration.

"I have great news for you guys," Willy went on to say as he led them farther into the house. "Remember when I told you how the women would outnumber the men four to one?"

The men nodded.

"Well, it's more like seven to one. I don't know if I gave the party planner the right guest book, but I swear there're more women here than I can shake a stick at. But, trust me, I'm going to try."

"You're a dirty old man." Marcel laughed.

Willy frowned. "You say that like it's a bad thing."

Just then a curvaceous woman decked in pink satin sashayed past the three men and each set of eyes trailed after the bounce of her backside.

"Lord have mercy." Willy removed his arms from the men's shoulders and reached inside his tux to remove one of his trademark Cuban cigars. "Let the interviewing process begin."

"You told your uncle?" Marcel glared at his best friend.

"Look around. Don't you think I need some help? Besides, they're his friends. He has the inside scoop on every one."

The last person Marcel wanted to select a date for him was Uncle Willy. Especially since he had a propensity to select borderline criminally insane women for himself.

Willy chuckled and removed his cigar. "I already have a few women in mind."

"No offense, Uncle Willy, but I prefer not to take anyone you've, uh, been out with."

"Ah. Good point." He tapped his chin. "No one wants sloppy seconds, right?"

Marcel forced a smile. "Something like that."

Willy winked. "The night is young. Let's get started."

Fashionably late, Nora stepped out of her leased Mercedes in a banana-yellow, full-sequined gown and matching Prada pumps that set her back a pretty penny. However, if everything went according to plan, she would go back to living the life of excess as she did in her modeling days.

At the door, she handed over her forged invitation and donned her yellow and silver mask and went in search of Casanova Brown.

When she crossed over the threshold, her eyes bulged at the sheer splendor of the house. The marble floors, Greek columns, and cathedral ceiling had Nora wondering, just who was this William Bassett and how did he come to own such a magnificent home?

"Lord have mercy. I must be dreaming," a man's bullhorn voice blared within inches of her ears.

Slowly, she turned. Not the least bit surprised that the voice belonged to a short, robust man with a wolfish grin. *I don't think so.*

His arms opened wide in greeting. "Welcome to my humble abode."

"You're William Bassett?"

"Shh." He pressed a finger against his lips. "We're not supposed to give out our identities, remember?"

"Right." Nora gave a slow nod, but mentally placed the aging playboy on her short list of backup plans.

He edged closer to her. "I have to admit that you've got the best body in the place."

She wiggled her hips as she met his beady gaze. "I have the best body, *period.*"

"Ah, modesty." He shoved a cigar into his mouth. "A woman after my own heart. You might be the type of woman my nephew's friend is looking for."

"Is that right?" Nora perked up. He had to be referring to Marcel.

"You're not here with anyone, are you?"

"I thought this was a singles party."

"It is, it is." He looped his meaty arm around her small waist. "But people have been known to break the rules from time to time. So it never hurts to double-check."

One of Nora's top ten rules of how to marry a millionaire prohibited her from burning bridges with any member of the millionaire club, so she overlooked the man's unwanted embrace and continued to smile at her plan B.

"So where is this friend of your nephew's?"

Marcel mingled in the crowd. When he ran across one of his employees from T&B Entertainment, he really didn't think anything of it. Then he recognized Selena, Erin, Paula, and then finally Chelsea. What was going on? Surely these women weren't friends of Uncle Willy.

He asked a couple of them to dance and used the opportunity to find out what was going on, though in the back of his mind he was starting to suspect.

Chelsea was the one who finally cracked under the pressure.

Instead of getting upset, Marcel was amused— flattered even. For the first time, he managed to relax. He was definitely not going to find his future wife at this party.

Suddenly, there was a loud murmur among the crowd, peppered with a few shocked gasps. People stopped dancing and Marcel turned and tried to see what was happening. When his eyes landed on a fiery temptress in silk and lace, it was love at first sight.

Twenty-one

Marcel's eyes roamed slowly over a dress that was fire-engine red with a V-neck that split clear to a beautiful navel. How the dress managed to stay in place over her twin assets was a mystery that he was willing to unravel.

"Excuse me," he whispered to Chelsea and then deserted her in the crowd. By the time he crossed the room, his enchanting goddess had attracted a swarm of men around her, all asking for the first dance.

He met her hazel-green stare with a confident smile, but it quickly disappeared when she linked her arm through the man's next to her and allowed him to direct her to the dance floor.

"Lucky bastard," one of the men she'd deserted grumbled.

"Well, I'm next," another one announced.

"Who says?" a man confronted.

Marcel ignored the brewing competition and instead kept his gaze locked on the woman who continued to turn heads. The back of her dress also dipped low and had a fan of lace just above her derriere.

He fingered his mandarin collar as the room's temperature skyrocketed.

The beauty's dance partner turned to her on the floor and looked uncertain as to where he should place his hands. She tossed back her head with a laugh, which Marcel strained his ears to hear.

He headed toward her with no plan as to what he would say once he'd reached his destination. His years of being the calm, cool Casanova Brown pumped him with a false confidence as he tapped her partner's shoulder.

The man turned, but Marcel locked gazes with the object of his desire. "Mind if I cut in?"

"I'm not finished dancing with her," the man hissed menacingly.

Marcel waited for her response, but she simply smiled and turned back to her partner.

The stranger took her back into his arms and tossed Marcel an angry glare.

For Marcel, this sort of rejection was a new and strange experience. Instead of being angry, he was intrigued.

"Ouch. That had to hurt," Solomon said as he followed Marcel off the dance floor.

"Have any idea who she is?"

"No clue. But I have to hand it to her, she definitely knows how to enter a room. All the men in here are just waiting for that dress to shift in any direction. You think she's a performer?"

He shrugged. "There's something familiar about her."

"Surely you're not going to use the 'haven't we met somewhere before?' line. It's bad enough that you've already been shot down once."

"Thanks."

Solomon slapped him on the back. "Don't mention it."

"Ah, there you two are," Willy blared.

Thinking that Willy might know or recognize the lady in red, Marcel turned with a wide grin only for it to flip upside down when he recognized the woman Willy tugged behind him.

"Since I saw how you crashed and burned a minute ago, I brought you someone who might turn your night around."

Nora turned up the wattage on her smile and tried not to shoot a daggered gaze at the woman who'd stolen the spotlight. "Hello, Marcel."

"Ah, ah, ah," Willy admonished him. "No names. I should start ejecting people who break the rules. Everyone should've picked a nickname for tonight."

"In that case," Nora said, "call me Sunshine."

Willy laughed. "Ah. How appropriate."

"And you?" Willy looked to Marcel.

"Casanova," Solomon answered for him.

"I hate that name," Marcel confessed.

"Well, it'll do for tonight," Willy said, pushing Marcel and Nora closer together. "Now, you two dance and try to get to know each other." He tugged Marcel by the sleeve so he would lean down as he whispered, "If you don't like this one, let me know. I might take her for myself."

Though he had no romantic feelings for Nora, Marcel wasn't crazy enough to subject her to the madness that was Willy Bassett.

"So what does a woman have to do to get a dance around here?" Nora asked, slinking closer.

Marcel automatically stepped back, but then decided that one dance wouldn't hurt. He would just have to be on his p's and q's around his ambitious employee. "I would be honored if you'd have this dance with me," he said.

All was not lost, Nora decided. The lady in red could just eat her heart out.

Diana watched as Marcel gathered a woman who looked like a giant banana into his arms and waltz onto the dance floor. That wasn't a part of her plan. He was supposed to linger in the shadows and sulk for a while as she danced with strangers.

Why did she listen to Tim? Now what was she supposed to do? Had she blown her only opportunity for the night?

Men love mysteries and challenges, she repeated in her head. *Remain aloof and standoffish.*

"I feel as though you're not listening to me," the man in her arms said.

"Excuse me?" *Damn. I'm supposed have a French accent.*

The man smiled from behind a mask that made him look as if an ostrich had exploded on his face. "Your mind is on someone else. Am I right?"

"I'm sorry," she whispered, looking over his shoulder to see if she could catch another glimpse of Marcel.

"It's all right. Just please tell me it wasn't that jerk that tried to cut in on us."

She grimaced and the man laughed.

"Should have known I would lose out to another tall, dark, and handsome type. One of these days, short, light-skinned, and chubby is going to make a comeback and then you'll be sorry."

Diana laughed. "You're a very nice man . . . ?"

He filled in the blank for her. "Alfred."

"No real names," she reminded him.

"I know. That's my party name for the night."

She tried to swallow her amusement, but continued to laugh at the charming man. "Well, Alfred, I'm sure any of the women here would be lucky to have you."

"Famous last words." He chuckled. "So shall I lead you over to the man you wore this dynamite dress for this evening?"

She glanced over his shoulder at Marcel and the knockout in his arms. "No. That won't be necessary. It looks like he's moved on."

Alfred turned to sneak a peek.

"Don't look," she whispered. "I don't want him to know we're talking about him."

He laughed. "You're new at this, aren't you?"

"At what?"

"At trying to make a man jealous."

She didn't know what to say.

"It's all right," he assured her. "Trust me when I say that you're way ahead of the curve just by wearing that dress."

Her cheeks burned with embarrassment. "I was so confident that I could pull this off. But now that I'm here . . ."

He gave her a kind smile. "I don't believe I'm about to do this, but . . . just follow my lead."

Before Diana had the chance to comprehend

what he was about to do, he glided her through a throng of people and stopped next to Marcel and his banana cream puff.

Tapping Marcel's shoulder, Alfred forced on an amicable smile and asked, "Mind if I cut in?"

Diana turned as well and her eyes clashed with a very angry Nora Gibson. The woman's declaration of winning Marcel echoed in Diana's head and she suddenly had a renewed sense of purpose.

"Be my guest," Marcel said, turning out of Nora's arms and gravitating toward Diana.

Nora gasped and then stomped her foot as Marcel and Diana drifted away.

"I believe your partner is upset with you," Diana was careful to say in a thick, breathy French accent.

Marcel lifted a surprised brow, but then slid on a small grin. "I'm sure that she'll be fine," he assured her. "I'm more interested in you right now."

"Is that so?" Relishing the way one of his hands pressed against her bare back and his intense gaze slowly traveled down her body, Diana shivered.

"First, let me introduce myself. I'm Marcel Taylor."

She smiled. "No real names, remember? At least until the end of the night."

"All right then." His gaze now locked on her lips. "What is your name for tonight?"

"Mayte," she said with a quiet smile. "I like the way it sounds."

He nodded and rolled the name around on his tongue. "It's exotic, much like yourself."

"Thank you."

"No. Thank you for wearing that dress."

Their gazes locked for so long, she was sure that he could see straight through her elaborate mask and fake contact lenses. Any second now he would push her away in either shock or anger.

"Why don't we go somewhere where we can hear ourselves think?" he asked.

She swallowed. The fear of rejection when he found out who she was had her seriously considering cutting her losses and hightailing it out of there. She only had to stay until midnight, she told herself. Surely she could continue this charade until then.

"Are you game?" he asked when she didn't respond.

She loved the way he looked at her. It was unlike the blatant lust in the eyes of the other men in the room. It held something more. "Sure," she said, keeping with her fake accent and fighting back her butterflies.

Marcel turned, sliding his arm around her waist. The smile he shared with her threatened to split his face in half as he glided her toward a back patio. More than ever, he was glad that Solomon had talked him into coming to this party. Life as he knew it was about to change and he embraced it gladly.

He glanced down at Mayte and shared a smile as they stepped out onto the patio, but discovered that it was just as crowded there as the dance floor. Instead, he directed her through the gardens and down toward one of the gazebos.

"I don't know about this," she said, glancing over her shoulder. "Perhaps we should stay with the party."

He stopped. "I would just like to spend some quiet time and try to get to know you. Not to mention," he added, reaching up and removing his mask, "this thing is bugging the heck out of me."

Mayte pressed a hand to her mask and stepped back. "We're not supposed to remove our masks."

His lips sloped to the side. "I like to think of rules as mere guidelines."

"I don't." She turned.

"Wait." His hand shot out to grasp her arm. "You don't have to take yours off if you don't want to. In fact nothing is going to happen . . . unless you want it to."

She stared up at him for a long while before she visibly relaxed and turned back to face him. "We play by the rules."

"As you like." He calmly placed his mask back on and she rewarded him with a smile.

Marcel sighed as his eyes roamed over her face. At that moment, she confirmed something his heart knew all along. The familiar shape of her lips, the sweet scent of vanilla, and the slightly off-centered nose sent his heart a-flutter. "Shall we?" he asked, offering his arm.

"We shall." She accepted his offer and allowed him to lead the way.

Twenty-two

Diana wasn't aware of the exact moment when she ceased to live in reality and exist only in what had to be a fantasy. Everything seemed so perfect—too perfect, in fact.

Glancing up into the heavens, she was blown away by the black velvety sky and all those billions of stars that twinkled like diamonds back at her. She drew in a deep breath and was invigorated by the night's cool, clean air.

"You seem happy," he commented, as they stepped up into the gazebo.

"I am happy," she said, glancing over. "Aren't you?"

"Ecstatic."

Though she couldn't see his eyes, she could feel his gaze on her. Never in her life had she felt so empowered, so in control, and so feminine at the same time.

"So, *Mayte*. Where have you been all my life?"

She laughed. "Is that your best line, Casanova?"

He straightened. "How did you know my name for this evening?"

Damn. She mentally scrambled for an answer. "Everyone knows Marcel's alter ego as Casanova Brown."

"Is that right?" He inched closer. "You shouldn't pay attention to rumors."

"Not even the ones about you being an excellent lover?"

"Well, except that one."

His rumble of laughter rushed against the shell of her ear and her toes tingled. "I better be careful around you," she said, moving away in order to clear her head.

"With you in that dress, I could say the same for myself."

She twirled around. "You like?"

"I love." He approached her again. "You really shouldn't have to ask."

His closeness muddled her thoughts.

"So what do you say you tell me a little about yourself?" he asked, taking her hands into his. "What do you do? Where do you stay? And please tell me that you're available."

Think, think. She mimicked the playful laugh Tim taught her, and then narrowed the remaining space between them so she could walk her fingers up his chest. "Tonight is supposed to be all about mystery. Now, you don't want to ruin that, do you?"

In answer, Marcel's head descended and captured her lips in the sweetest kiss she'd ever known. Everything about him was like magic, from the way he brought her body to life to the way he influenced her imagination.

His passion overwhelmed her as she struggled

to get as close as possible to his heat. She'd dreamed of this moment for so long. She was afraid that it wasn't really happening. Her hand slid up and around his neck and she was lost.

How such a strong man could have such soft hands eluded Diana, but they sure felt heavenly as they roamed along her bare back. What would it be like to have them touching other places?

The sound of footsteps and laughter ended their short voyage to heaven as their lips sprang apart.

"Ah." Uncle Willy's voice cracked the air. "I didn't know anyone was out here." He draped his arms around two women and they all joined them inside the gazebo. "But I guess I should have known that you'd try to get this pretty little filly alone. Of course, between the two of us we could get our own private party started. What do you say?"

Diana's eyes bulged. Surely he didn't mean what she thought he meant.

Marcel hugged Diana close. "We'll pass." He guided her away from their new guests.

"Can't say that I blame you." Willy laughed. "You know you're more than welcome to give her a tour around the rest of the house. If you know what I mean."

"I'll keep that in mind." Marcel and Diana stepped out of the gazebo and headed back toward the house.

Diana waited until they were out of earshot before she whispered, "Does that sort of thing happen a lot with you two?"

"Does what happen?" he asked with a hint of surprise in his voice.

She stopped and glanced up. It was difficult to

meet his dark gaze in the black night. "Do you two share women?" She could feel his laughter rumble through his body.

"Never. What do you think I am—some kind of devil or something?"

Diana's breath hitched as her mind instantly went to the costume she had picked out for him. Did he know?

"Why?" he asked. "Were you interested in his offer?"

"Hell, no." Her body stilled as she spoke her outrage. She had also forgotten her accent for a moment. Her heart hammered in her chest, while she suddenly felt exposed.

"Well, that's good to know," he finally said, and then continued to lead her toward the house.

Soon, they were among a cluster of people and once again, Diana drew everyone's attention.

Marcel retrieved two flutes of champagne from a passing waiter but before he could hand one to Diana, Solomon appeared at her side.

"I absolutely must have a dance with the most beautiful creature here. Shall we?" he asked, offering her his arm.

Diana hesitated, but at seeing Marcel's irritation, she decided, *What the hell?* and accepted his arm. "I'd love to."

Solomon winked at Marcel and led Diana off to the dance floor. "That ought to burn his hide," he whispered.

"Are you angry with him?" she asked, returning to her French accent.

"Of course not. That's my man right there."

Diana glanced up at him.

"I don't mean that he's my *man* man."

She laughed at how his mocha complexion darkened with embarrassment. "It's okay, you know. I have plenty of gay friends," she teased him.

"No, no. We're not gay." His neck was now a bright red. "I just meant that we're best friends."

"Oh." She exaggerated her understanding. "That's good to know."

He took her into his arms and began swaying to the music. "You know, I'm helping my good buddy find his potential wife tonight."

So it's true. "I wouldn't have imagined he needed help in that department."

"He doesn't need help finding women. It's finding the right woman."

"And you're an expert in this area?" she asked.

"Well, uh, no." He frowned.

Diana smiled. "Interesting." From the corner of her eyes, she saw Marcel leaning against a Greek column as he watched them.

"What makes you think he's ready to settle down?" she asked.

Solomon shrugged. "He told me. Said he wanted what his parents have. They've been married for forty years."

Being a child of unmarried parents, Diana could only imagine what it would be like to be married to someone for so long. What kind of husband would Marcel Taylor make?

For the past two years, Diana had looked down her nose at her boss's promiscuous lifestyle while she battled her growing affection. Could she truly be the kind of woman he'd want to settle down with for the rest of his life?

Solomon cut into her thoughts to ask, "So does this beautiful woman have a name?"

"Mayte," she informed him.

"Good one," he said. "Now that I've told you my agenda for this evening, why don't you tell me about yourself?"

She drew in a deep breath and flashed him one of her best smiles. "All you need to know is that I'm here to have a good time. My past is of no importance and tomorrow will take care of itself."

Their gazes met and Solomon joined her in a smile.

"A woman of mystery. My buddy should love that."

"Enough about your friend. What about you? Why aren't you looking for a wife yourself?"

Solomon appeared stunned to have the tables turned on him. "My search ended a long time ago," he said honestly. "She's a tall, bronzed beauty with eyes the color of honey."

Diana blinked. The description conjured the image of the woman who'd come to see Marcel a few weeks ago. "So, you're in love?"

"Have been for most of my life. One of these days, I'm going to dredge up the nerve to tell her."

"You know, my grandmother told me something that I think you need to hear," she said, giving him a kind smile.

"Oh?"

"She said that a life full of regrets is no life at all."

Their dancing slowed as Solomon stared at her. "She sounds like a wise woman."

"Yes. She is."

A hand appeared suddenly and tapped Solomon's shoulder. "Mind if I cut in?" a man with a mask that resembled a lion's head asked.

In the next moment, Diana was whisked away. A few minutes later, another man stepped in, and then another. So much attention was quickly going to her head and filling her with an awesome sense of power.

While she continued to dance with her many suitors, Marcel lingered in the background and watched her every move. When she found herself back in Solomon's arms, Marcel's patience finally ran out.

"You've had her long enough," he said, tapping Solomon on the shoulder.

Solomon laughed as he released Diana to him. "I was wondering how long it would take for you to cut in."

"Too long," Marcel said, his eyes locked on her. "How about that tour now?"

"I'd be delighted."

Marcel offered her his arm and together they deserted Solomon on the dance floor.

"So how do you know so much about this house?" Diana asked as they moved through the crowd.

"I've been here on a few occasions."

"But not to share women?"

He tossed a smile over at her. "You sure seem interested in my love life."

They started up the staircase, while Diana thought of her rebuttal. "It's not a crime for a woman to be curious, is it?"

"No," he said, reaching the top landing. "But I thought that the night was supposed to be one of great mystery." He drew her to him. "That's what you wanted, wasn't it?"

He was staring at her again and she fought the urge to remove her mask. Playing games was never her forte; however, her fear returned and a long list of what-ifs scrambled her brain, the main one being: what if he rejected her? What would she do then?

"So what should we see first?" she asked, ignoring his question.

"Why don't we just walk around and see where we end up?"

The sentence was innocent, but his eyes weren't and Diana was suddenly aware that the game had just moved to the next level.

Twenty-three

Diana was more than impressed with the layout of William Bassett's home. However, being accustomed to pinching pennies, she couldn't understand why bachelors like Mr. Bassett and Marcel needed so much space.

"And this room," Marcel said, clicking on a light switch, "is one of my all-time favorites."

The lighting was, at best, a dim glow, but upon seeing a Jacuzzi in the middle of the room, she understood what he meant.

He leaned down and whispered in her ear. "How about we get a little wet?"

Diana's body tingled at the thought. "We didn't bring suits."

"I won't tell anyone if you won't." He grinned at her as his fingers boldly skimmed the exposed valley between her breasts. "I'm very good at keeping secrets."

She sucked in her breath while his dark gaze trapped her own. "I—I don't know."

A corner of his lips sloped. "You don't trust me?"

She swallowed, but the lump in her throat refused to budge. "I didn't say that."

"Your eyes did." His fingers now lifted to run along the edge of her mask. "I'm not going to force you to do anything you don't want. You can trust me on that, *Mayte.*"

"I do." He wasn't the problem. The question was whether she trusted herself.

"Good." He turned around and closed the bedroom door. The room immediately darkened.

Diana, however, cleared her head to assess exactly what she'd gotten herself into.

"The first thing we need is to do away with these." Marcel removed his mask and then reached for hers.

She jumped back. "I'll do it." She reached up with shaky fingers and a pounding heart. She removed the mask and then watched a smile blossom across Marcel's face.

"A mask beneath a mask," he said. "Clever."

Diana sighed with relief. Tim had come up with the great idea of creating a replica of her mask with makeup on her face. It was meant for the unlikely event her mask broke or fell off.

"Now, let's see if I can get you out of these clothes."

She took another step back. "You go first."

His smile broadened. "If you insist."

When he reached for the top button of his tux, Diana was mesmerized. His fingers moved in slow motion while the room's temperature escalated.

A few minutes later, and at the first flash of skin, Diana was sweltering. A renegade thought that she was in over her head raced across her mind, but the rest of her refused to turn back now.

With his jacket and shirt gone, Marcel's hand then went to his pants. "Any moment now, I expect you to start stuffing dollar bills into my briefs," he joked.

She smiled, while her boldness grew by leaps and bounds. "That depends on if I like what I see."

"I love a woman with a sense of humor," he said.

Diana's hackles stood at attention. Once again, she felt exposed, but she managed to convince herself she was overreacting.

Marcel's pants hit the floor, and then his black briefs were next.

Despite the room's dim lighting, Diana had no trouble making out Marcel's size and length and the only word that came to mind was, "Beautiful."

His smile grew wicked. "Thank you, but I believe it's your turn now."

Her gaze snapped back to his as her heart leaped into her throat. Fear tackled her at all angles. What had she done? She'd only been with one man in her entire life and performing a semistriptease was not included.

"Do you need help?"

She didn't respond—she couldn't.

"Have you changed your mind?"

He asked the question with such tenderness and concern it brought her complex emotions to the forefront. She came there tonight to grab his attention, flirt behind the safety of a mask, and then disappear into the night. Now, she realized it was all a lie. She came there for this moment—to make love to a man that caused many sleepless nights.

Diana's hands stopped trembling and she reached

behind her to unsnap the lone button just above her butt and beneath the fan of lace. She tugged with more strength than was necessary and the button fell to the floor.

"Ohmigosh." She stepped back and looked around.

Marcel took her hands in his and once again his gaze stole her attention. "Don't worry about it. We'll look for it later." He pulled her close before his eyes deserted hers to fall to her gown. His hands lifted the thin material across her shoulder and then skimmed down to the open V-cut.

"Before we go any further, I want to make sure this is something you want to do."

It was hard enough for Diana to breathe, let alone try to speak, but when his eyes returned to hers again, she found her voice. "I'm positive."

With those words, Marcel's head descended and their lips met in another sweet kiss of surrender. The electricity pouring into her body was as if she'd been plugged into an electrical socket, glowing from the inside out. This was a whole new emotion for her. She couldn't recall anything that even came close.

Marcel pushed the straps from her shoulders, and the gown fell effortlessly to the floor.

Fantasy became reality when Marcel's strong but soft fingers caressed her shoulders, her back, and the sensitive curves along her hips. She shivered against his feathery touch, but inched closer until her breasts pressed against his hard chest and her knees threatened to give way.

If Marcel had any doubts about seducing his secretary, they all melted away at the feel of her nipples against him. His hands flew to them as if by some magnetic pull and they were just as he remembered—one slightly bigger than the other.

He gave them a gentle squeeze and then swallowed her responsive sigh. He was definitely going through with this. His heart and soul demanded it.

Drunk with passion, he moved his lips from hers to explore other parts of her body. Their short journey down the column of her neck elicited more moans, but when they settled on an erect nipple, her ragged gasp was music to his ears.

Diana dragged her fingers through his hair and kneaded the muscles of his back while she continued to plunge further into a pool of euphoria. Tonight would hold no regrets, she vowed, and she would remember this night for as long as she lived.

Marcel continued his gentle sucking while his hands slid her lacy panties from her hips. When they fell to her feet, she kicked them and her shoes off. Now nothing stood between them.

"How about we get in that Jacuzzi now?" he asked, pulling away.

Diana blinked through the cloud of confusion before his question penetrated, but by that time he was already leading her toward the center of the room.

He pushed a button with his toe and the water whirled to life. "After you," he said, gesturing her to take the first step.

Determined to live out the rest of this fantasy night, Diana stepped into the warm, soothing water and he followed in after her.

He sat in one of the corners and then beckoned her toward him. She came to him without hesitation. With some work, he instructed her on how to straddle him, but without consummating the unison just yet.

Instead, while he had her beautiful twins before him, he resumed his previous suckling.

Diana rolled her head back in ecstasy and, once again, surrendered to Marcel completely. As she enjoyed his hot mouth, her eyes snapped open at the sudden feel of his hands rubbing along her inner thigh, her feminine lips, and then the pulsing bud between her legs.

A low moan of pleasure escaped her as her body trembled restlessly for what was just beyond her reach.

Marcel drew his mouth away from her breasts just as her lips lowered to take possession of his. Their tongues entangled in a sweet duet of passion and need, while his hand never ceased its intimate caress.

She came undone as her hips rocked in sync with his hand's rhythm and in no time her first orgasm spread through her body like a wildfire.

Marcel gasped as her nails dug deeper into his shoulders, but she couldn't release her hold until the final shock wave left her body.

Watching Diana's reaction only deepened Marcel's love for his usually reclusive secretary. There was something remarkably exotic at seeing her put aside her inhibitions. Plus, it was sexy as hell to watch the unguarded emotions on her face.

The second mask of face paint or makeup truly did a lousy job at hiding her identity, but Marcel had no intentions of telling her as much. He was enjoying this fantasy she'd created and he was hell-bent on making sure that she enjoyed it, too.

Just when Diana was beginning to control her

breathing again, Marcel lifted her from the water and sat her on the edge of the Jacuzzi. He laid her down and while he continued to rain kisses along her neck and the valley between her breasts, he carefully positioned himself between her legs.

Diana became mindless to her surroundings, her circumstances, and even her elaborate charade. Her thoughts were consumed with the extraordinary pleasure Marcel gave her body.

The moment his tongue entered her, Diana's whimpers and moans filled the room like music. He controlled the tempo and the beat of the melodic sounds just by the rhythm he set with his oral worship.

It wasn't long before she was climbing the walls with her next orgasm and Marcel just barely saved himself from being crushed between her thighs.

"Careful." He chuckled.

Diana's face burned with embarrassment. "Sorry."

As much as he enjoyed watching and pleasuring Diana, it was becoming increasingly harder for Marcel to ignore his erection. It throbbed to the point of being painful and he could no longer deny how much he wanted her—how much he needed her.

He picked her up and managed to step out of the Jacuzzi with the ease of Mr. Olympia lifting a fifty-pound dumbbell. Their wet bodies were quickly sprawled across the bed's silk sheets as their lips merged in an explosive kiss.

The heat of Marcel's touch ruled every inch of Diana's body. She clung to him, whimpering as his hands returned to the slick passage between her legs. His name fell from her lips like a religious chant as her body strained for an end to his erotic torture.

The pressure building inside Marcel was unbearable, while he extended the foreplay by touching and kissing to the point of madness—both hers and his. When he couldn't wait any longer, he scrambled for his pants that were strewn beside the bed on the floor. He withdrew a few condoms from his wallet and then returned.

Diana helped sheath his impressive member, but then surprised him by climbing on top to take the dominant position. He held his breath as she slowly slid down his shaft until he filled her completely. For a few heart-pounding moments, she didn't move.

He waited patiently, and when she started to rock, he rolled his head and eyes back at the exquisite feel of her. In no time, Marcel relinquished the role as seducer and Diana sent him on a roller coaster of emotions he'd never experienced.

Her liquid heat was more than he could handle and before he knew it, his gasps and groans drowned out her sighs and whimpers. It was an exquisite agony as her thighs tightened around him.

Marcel's sole agenda was to fulfill and satisfy this magnificent woman, yet he was powerless to stop the all-consuming demands of his own body. His hands locked onto her hips to help accelerate the rhythm. When that wasn't enough, he quickly flipped her onto her back and took over the dominant position and drove his point home.

His thrusts weren't slow and measured, as he would've liked, but hard and urgent. She raised her knees to take him in deeper. Her inner walls held him, squeezed him until his breathing became short and choppy.

Their cries of release echoed throughout the

room as both swore fireworks exploded behind their closed eyes.

Never in Diana's wild imagination did she think that such bliss was possible. The gentle hum of her body made her feel as though she was in tune with the world around her. The sheer beauty of what she'd just experienced brought tears to her eyes.

Marcel pulled her close for a brief snuggle, but before long he began to pepper kisses along her neck, shoulder, and then her collarbone. In the next moment they were ready for round two.

It was the best Diana had ever felt and more than she'd expected. There were times when he'd brought her to the verge of tears and at other times she giggled like a teenager. It was a wonderful night—a beautiful night.

Sometime after the third round, Diana woke with a jolt in Marcel's arms. *What time is it?* She glanced around the room in search of a clock. She had the sinking feeling that it was past midnight and Jimmy had probably left.

Beside her, Marcel slept snoring lightly. She gently pried herself away from him and slinked away from the bed. Again she wondered what time it was, but couldn't find a clock in the room. She gathered her dress and panties from the floor and then rushed into the bathroom to put them on. She soon discovered that with the missing button, the back of her dress hung open like a hospital gown. She couldn't walk out like that.

She rolled her eyes heavenward at her unbelievable luck and then glanced in the mirror. She nearly screamed out in fright at seeing that half of her makeup had smeared, exposing her identity.

Had Marcel noticed? No, she assured herself. He would have said something. Right?

She shook off the frightening thought and tried to figure out how she was going to get out of there.

"Okay, just go out and put on the other mask," she whispered aloud, but she had no clue as to how she was going to fix her dress.

She peeked out of the bathroom door and was pleased to see that Marcel was still curled up fast asleep on the bed. Her gaze lowered to the floor to his tux and she had an idea.

A few minutes later, dressed in Marcel's large tux and with her mask back on, Diana snuck outside through the room's French doors with her clothes and shoes clutched in her arms. She was grateful that the entire second floor shared a wraparound balcony. When she reached the east wing, she found a great spot to climb down. Halfway down, however, she discovered it wasn't so great and nearly broke her neck.

On the ground, she cowered in the shadows until she reached the area where the cars were parked. Only then did she get a good view of the party that was still in full swing. Now, if she could just find Jimmy.

She crept among the cars, ducking whenever she thought she was close to being exposed. At long last, she saw Jimmy pacing near one of the limousines in front of the line. She breathed a sigh of relief, and ran barefoot across the lush lawn.

Jimmy glanced up and his face twisted in confusion when he recognized the masked woman, but not what she was wearing.

"How late am I?" she whispered, reaching him.

He frowned. "It's almost one. I'll be lucky if I don't lose my job over this."

"I'm so sorry, but let's get out of here."

"Where have you been? Is everything all right?" he asked as he rushed to open the back door.

"I'll tell you once we're on our way." She dove into the backseat.

"Yes, ma'am." He closed the door.

Diana plopped her clothes down next to her, and then twisted in her seat to stare back at the house as they drove away. She breathed a sigh of relief. She'd pulled off the impossible: she'd stolen one night with the man of her dreams.

So why wasn't she happy?

Marcel dreamed that he and Diana were getting married in the Bahamas. He stretched out to pull her close, but when his hands fell to the cold and vacant spot next to him, he was instantly awake. "Diana?"

The bed was empty.

He tossed the sheets from his body and climbed out of bed. The bathroom door was open and when he peeked inside, it was empty as well. He couldn't have been asleep long, he reasoned. Twenty minutes tops.

"I don't believe this," he mumbled under his breath. It was proving difficult not to feel as though he'd been used. He'd played along with Diana's game thinking that at the end of the night she would reveal her identity. He would've acted surprised, and then continued making love for the rest of the night. He didn't think she would pull a Houdini on him.

He walked out of the bathroom and noticed that the French doors were cracked open. A smile passed his lips as he headed in that direction, but once he pulled it open, his smile disappeared.

"She's gone," he declared with disbelief. He closed the door and then stared at it for a long while. After thinking about it for a moment, he convinced himself she'd just gone downstairs, perhaps to get something to drink.

He liked the idea and started to bob his head at the logic behind it. He turned to retrieve his clothing so he could make sure another man didn't detain her from returning, but his clothes were gone.

"No, she didn't," he whispered. He turned up the lighting in the room and searched every inch of the place. The only things he could find were his shoes, his briefs, and one high-heeled sandal by the French doors.

"Damn."

Twenty-four

Diana and Jimmy returned the limousine without incident and he promptly drove her home in his old beat up Ford Ranger. Whatever magic the night had provided earlier had long disappeared.

Diana told the truth about her clothes and the button that had snapped off. Thankfully, he was too much of a gentleman to ask where the tuxedo came from. By the time she made it home, it was close to three A.M.

She knew before she opened the door that Tim and her grandmother would be up in the living room with a barrage of questions. However, as wonderful as her time with Marcel had been, she wasn't in the mood to rehash the night's events.

Giving Jimmy a final wave, Diana quickly rushed to her apartment. When she entered, she was surprised by the darkness and the silence. She closed and locked the door behind her, and then walked to the living room to make sure that no one had waited up for her.

It was empty.

Since it was so late, maybe they just assumed that she wasn't coming home. She wondered why she was so bothered by that. Moments ago she was dreading seeing them, and now she was disappointed.

"I'm just tired," she mumbled, and then headed off to bed. Minutes later, stripped of Marcel's suit, and her face scrubbed clean, Diana stared up at the ceiling with a broken heart.

Now that she'd indulged in her fantasy, what was next? How could she go back to just being Marcel's dutiful secretary? The answer was obvious: she couldn't.

"Why didn't I just dance with him and leave like I was supposed to?" she continued to question herself. Her original plan was for harmless flirtation. She had no idea how she made the giant leap to being a shameless hussy.

She eased onto her side and realized she was being too hard on herself, but turning off the voice of her worst critic became damn near impossible.

After roaming the second story of Uncle Willy's large home wrapped in a silk sheet, Marcel kept thinking that someone hovering in the shadows was catching all of this on video. He made it to Willy's master bedroom and found a pair of sweat clothes that were too short and too large, but he crammed into them anyway.

He thought about putting his shoes back on, but thought the outfit with dress shoes was a little over the top. The next problem was getting out there without being seen. It was nearly four A.M. and the party was still in full swing. His mind filled with questions about where Solomon was at the moment, but he had no plans to search for him in his present getup.

Instead he picked up the phone next to Willy's bed and dialed the limousine's mobile number.

When Charlie's gruff voice came on the line, Marcel had no doubts that he'd woke him up. He quickly instructed Charlie to meet him on the east wing of the house with the limo and then left the bedroom through the French doors.

Racing down the long balcony, he hoped no one roaming the grounds or, worse, someone using one of the bedrooms saw him. He found a spot to climb down and threw his leg over the banister.

That's where his luck ended.

One minute he was balancing his weight on the ledge, and in the next he hit the ground with one of his ankles folding like paper.

Diana woke the next morning to the rich aroma of Folgers coffee wafting throughout the house. Glancing over at the clock, she saw that she'd only been asleep for a couple of hours. She groaned and snuggled deeper beneath the covers.

Her brief sanctuary crashed to a halt at the sound of the light rap on her door. She squeezed her eyes shut and prayed her visitor would go away.

However, the door's slow creak told her that wasn't happening.

"Diana, are you awake?" Louisa's soft, lilting voice floated to her.

Diana didn't answer, but instead of her grandmother leaving, she grew louder. "Diana?"

Sighing, Diana tossed the covers back from her head. "Yes?"

"Oh, good. You're awake." She crossed farther into the room and sat on the corner of the bed. "I want to hear everything. Don't leave anything out."

"Is she awake?" Tim asked from the door.

Diana groaned. "Guys, not now. I need to get some more sleep." She grabbed the covers again and buried her head.

Louisa was having none of that and dragged the covers back from Diana's body. "Come on. We're dying to know how our work paid off. Though I suspect it went well. We waited up until two."

"Yeah. I thought Jimmy had to have the limo back by twelve-thirty?"

"We were late." Diana grudgingly sat up. It pained her to see their eager faces because they clearly wanted to know more than she was willing to share.

"Here, I brought you some coffee." Tim held out a mug.

Flashing a smile of gratitude, she accepted the warm mug. She took a few sips while Tim claimed another spot on the bed.

Their anxious faces slowly showed signs of impatience.

"We're ready whenever you are," Louisa said, patting Diana's leg. "What happened when you made your grand entrance?"

Diana recalled the moment with a smile. "All eyes were on me."

Louisa giggled. "Ah, if it was anything like the old days, I bet you felt fabulous."

"Yeah, I did." She continued grinning. "That was the first time anything like that has ever happened to me."

Her grandmother reached for her hand. "I'm so happy to have helped passed this torch."

Diana laughed. "I can't say you've never done anything for me."

"Okay. So what happened when Mr. Gorgeous spotted you?" Tim wanted to know.

"The world melted away," she admitted without thinking.

Tim and Louisa glanced at each other and smiled.

As for the rest of the evening, Diana recalled everything but the private tour of the Bassett mansion. As far as her makeover team was concerned the night was a success.

By some miracle she was able to suppress her melancholy while she told them what they wanted to hear.

After breakfast and when Tim had gone home, Louisa approached Diana and tried to get to the bottom of what she wasn't saying.

"It's nothing," Diana said, donning her sweat clothes.

"You're going jogging?"

"I need to clear my head."

Louisa crossed her arms. "Why can't you tell me what's bothering you? You had fun last night, right?"

"I had a wonderful time," Diana said, avoiding her gaze. "It was perfect."

"Right up to the moment you slept with him?"

Diana's gaze snapped up.

"Oh, don't look so shocked." Louisa waved her off. "I can read you like a book." She winced and then clutched at her stomach.

"Are you all right?" Diana reached to steady her. "Come on, let's go in the living room where you can sit down." She dutifully helped her grandmother to the sofa. When she reached for the phone, Louisa stopped her.

"I'm okay."

Diana wasn't buying it.

"Really, I'm fine. I want to talk about you."

"My problems aren't important."

"You're important to me." She squeezed her hand. "Now, tell me what's going on with you."

They held each other's gaze for a long while before Diana finally gave up.

"It was a mistake. I shouldn't have slept with him."

"Didn't you use protection?"

Diana rolled her eyes. "Yes, but that's not the issue."

"What is the issue?"

"I'm just another notch on Casanova's bedpost. Sleeping with him wasn't what I went there for. A man isn't interested in a woman he can get in the sack within two hours of meeting her. I came off as easy."

"Now, you don't know that."

"Oh, come on, Nana. I blew it."

"We don't know that yet. I say we move into phase two. When you return to work, let's see what happens. I'm sure this morning he's interviewing half the people at that party trying to find out the identity of the mystery woman in red."

"Return to work? Are you crazy?" Diana jumped to her feet and began pacing. "I can't go back there."

"Why not?"

She stopped and frowned down at Louisa. "What gives you the impression that I'm some great actress? I can't go back to working beside him every day or even looking him in the eye without remembering what happened last night."

"That good, huh?"

Diana's hands balled at her sides.

"All right, all right," Louisa said before her granddaughter exploded. "Then just tell him it was you."

Stunned, Diana stared at her. "Is that supposed to be a joke?"

Louisa sighed. "You *were* planning to tell him eventually, right?"

"Yeah, but that was before I left my dignity next to a Jacuzzi."

Her grandmother's eyes lit up. "A Jacuzzi? Wow."

"Focus, Nana."

"Fine. So what do you plan to do?"

Diana crossed her arms and lifted her chin with determination. "The only thing I can do. I'm quitting my job."

On Monday, Marcel hobbled into work with crutches and his right leg in a cast. It didn't take a rocket scientist to figure out that he was the reason women were whispering whenever he passed them in the hallways.

The racket he had made at the Bassett estate when he broke his ankle drew a lot of unwanted attention. Then, of course, there was the outfit and the missing woman in red. Bottom line, the rumor mill was in full swing with him taking center stage.

"Marcel," Solomon called out and quickly caught up with him before he was about to escape into his office. "Your father is in there."

It's going to be one of those days. "How long has he been in there?"

Solomon glanced at his watch. "A few minutes." At Marcel's pained expression, he added, "If it makes you feel better, I think he's in a good mood."

"Well, that makes one of us." Marcel swung his crutches into gear and continued limping to his office. As he passed Diana's empty desk, his heart contracted painfully, but he ignored it.

As he entered his office, both his father and mother jumped to their feet with wide smiles, but they quickly disappeared when their eyes fell to Marcel's leg.

"Oh, honey. What happened?" Camille rushed over to him.

"I'm fine." He stepped into his mother's embrace while he balanced on his crutches. His mother's beauty never ceased to amaze him. She was a five-foot-five knockout with beautiful silver hair whose active lifestyle helped her remain fit.

"Been playing ball again, son?" Donald asked.

Son? He was in a good mood. "What are you two doing here?"

"We came here to thank you," his mother said.

"Thank me?"

Donald moved over to Camille and draped a loving arm around her shoulder. "You putting me on that plane to France saved our marriage." He kissed her.

An instant smile caressed Marcel's lips. "That's great. So everything is okay?"

"Everything is wonderful." Camille stretched her arms around Donald's waist.

"I just realized that I was being an old fool and if I didn't straighten out I was going to lose the best thing that ever happened to me," Donald said.

"That's great to hear." Marcel's smile beamed and his chest swelled with pride. This was one load off his mind. Maneuvering his way around his glowing parents, he hobbled over to his desk.

"Anyway, we came by to ask you a question," Camille said, and then nudged Donald to talk.

"Yeah. I came by to see if you'd like to be the best man when your mom and I renew our vows."

Marcel fell into his seat. "You're renewing your vows?"

Donald's face ballooned into the widest smile Marcel had ever witnessed, but there was no doubt that it was genuine.

"We have you to thank," Donald said.

Marcel didn't know what to make of so many compliments from a man who'd been so stingy with them throughout his life. "I'm glad I could help. What kind of compromise did you two work out?"

"Your father is going to find a hobby. He's thinking about trying golf again."

"That's an expensive hobby," Marcel reminded him.

Donald winked. "I can afford it."

Marcel stared at them, completely stunned by what a jaunt around the world could accomplish. He was also a little jealous.

"For a man who knows so much about relationships," his father began, "maybe you really should stop playing the field like you said and settle down." Donald winked.

"Oh. Grandchildren," Marcel's mother added. "That would be wonderful." Her voice lowered to a whisper. "You know, I've always liked that Diana. Where is she, by the way?"

"A leave of absence," Marcel said as Diana's image floated to mind and his heart squeezed again. What was going to happen when she returned to work? If she returned.

Every woman in the office had one question on her mind: who was the mysterious woman in red? Nora was no exception. The woman had pulled off an incredible feat that included placing Marcel Taylor in a compromising position. At least that's what everyone thought since Taylor apparently misplaced his tuxedo.

Nora was ready to throw in the towel. She couldn't remember working so hard to win a man. It was embarrassing. On her way back to her office, she stopped in the break room for a coffee refill. Casually, she passed the company's bulletin board and looked at the many pictures pinned up from picnics and Christmas parties.

When she came across a picture of Diana, she couldn't pull her eyes away from the shape of her face and mouth. Before long, Nora mentally placed the mask of the femme fatale over the docile secretary. "I'll be damned."

The glass slipper

Twenty-five

Long after his parents left, Marcel answered all calls on the first ring hoping each time it would be Diana on the other end. When Solomon popped in toward the end of the day, Marcel held Diana's letter of resignation in one hand while nursing a rum and Coke in the other.

"You really need to get a temp for Diana. There's a pile of paper stacking up on her desk."

Marcel nodded absently.

Solomon eased into the chair across from the desk and propped his feet up. "Plus everyone is running around naked out in the office."

Marcel nodded again.

"Damn. You really have it bad."

"Huh?" Marcel finally pulled his gaze away from the letter.

Solomon laughed. "You haven't heard a word I've said."

"Sorry." Marcel lowered the letter onto his desk

and, after only two sips, pushed his drink aside. "I got a feeling she's not coming back."

Lost, Solomon frowned. "Who? Diana?"

Marcel's eyes fell to the letter again. "Yeah. Don't ask me how I know."

"Well, that was going to be my next question."

"I don't want her to leave me," Marcel confessed, and then slowly dragged his gaze up to meet Solomon's. "I'm in love with her."

Solomon's mouth sagged opened. "But what about the woman from the party the other night? I thought you had a strong connection with her."

"She fooled you too?"

At the knock on the door, Marcel yelled for the visitor to enter.

"Hello, Mr. Taylor," Lee Castleman said, as he entered the office. He smiled as his sharp blue eyes sparkled. "Sorry I couldn't get here sooner, but my whole team is working on one heck of a case."

Solomon stood with a frown.

"You don't have to leave," Marcel said. "Castleman is just delivering something for me."

"Yeah, I was kind of surprised that you wanted me to do research on Ms. Guy, but here you go." Castleman handed over a folder.

"Thanks."

"Don't mention it. I'll just put it on your tab." He turned and left the room as quickly as he'd entered.

Solomon looked at his friend as he sat down. "What was all that about?"

"The mysterious *Mayte*."

He frowned. "But I thought Castleman said . . . You don't mean . . . ?" Solomon floundered. "You have to be kidding me." He stood from the chair again.

"Nope."

"Diana Guy? Where in the hell did she get a body like that?"

"She's had it all along. Trust me. Whenever she wears a skirt, I've noticed she has these strong calves you could probably bounce a quarter off of. I bet she's a runner."

Solomon laughed and shook his head. "When it comes to women, nothing gets past you, does it?"

"A few things. Like I don't understand the point of her coming to the party like that and for us to . . . well, I guess I don't understand why she left the way she did. No note, no phone call or anything. We had this amazing night and then she just disappears."

"You're waiting for the morning-after call?"

Marcel blinked. "No, it's just—"

"I can't believe my ears. A woman actually has Casanova Brown waiting by the phone. You're whipped."

"I'm not whipped."

Solomon cracked an imaginary whip and then collapsed in a fit of laughter back into the chair.

Marcel rolled his eyes. "Can we get back to my problem? Diana isn't coming back. I just know it."

"Then go talk to her. Isn't that what you're always telling me to do?"

"It's not that simple."

"Ah, sounds like something I've said."

"No offense, but I'm nothing like you."

"But you got what you wished for, right? You wanted what I had. You know *who* you want. Now what?"

Marcel shrugged as his gaze once again fell to the letter.

After a long silence, Solomon spoke up. "A wise woman once said: a life full of regrets is no life at all."

"Who said that?"

"Mayte's grandmother . . . or rather Diana's."

"Louisa Styles." A wide smile stretched across Marcel's lips. "You know, she's right."

For the next five weeks, Diana decided that the best way to keep her mind off her troubles was to keep busy. She spent time with her grandmother at the park, took in a few movies, and charged a couple of expensive meals to Mr. Visa.

Today she dedicated herself to clean every inch of the house. She washed and waxed the car, and then set out to cook a three-course meal for dinner.

"Has she been like this all day?" Tim asked Louisa while he helped set the table.

"I'm afraid so. I think she's worse off than before we talked her into going to that blasted ball."

"I really wish you two wouldn't talk like I wasn't here," Diana said, placing the salad bowl on the table.

"Sorry," Tim said. "But she's right, you know. I'm sorry we talked you into going."

Caleb frowned as he set out the glasses. "Tim, I thought you said she had a good time."

"I did." Diana shrugged.

"But you're going to quit your job."

"I've been thinking about it for a long time, so

don't beat yourself up. I'll go in to work tomorrow and turn in my thirty-day notice." She didn't have a clue as to how she was going to work beside Marcel even for that short amount of time.

"Have you been able to find something else?" Caleb asked. "You know the market is kind of rough now."

"Yeah, I know." She sighed. She had been looking and calling around. She was beginning to think that she was being blackballed or something. The few positions she found couldn't match her current salary and she couldn't afford to take a pay cut. "I'm still looking."

There was no point in considering relocating. Louisa was born in Georgia and she vowed to die there as well.

The phone rang.

"I wonder who that is," Diana said.

Louisa shrugged as she placed the basket of bread on the table.

After the second ring, Louisa turned toward it. "I'll get it."

Diana went back into the kitchen for the lasagna. Her mind was already on doing dishes after dinner when she returned to the dining room. When she did, she quickly noticed that everyone looked as though they'd witnessed a murder. "What is it?"

"It's for you," Louisa whispered. "It's Marcel."

Her heart dropped. She wasn't ready to deal with him just yet. She had a whole night to prepare to see him again, much less talk to him. "Tell him I'm not here," she whispered.

"I already told him you were," Louisa said with her hand over the mouthpiece.

Diana cursed under her breath, but still didn't want to take the call.

"It's probably just business," Louisa said. "No big deal."

Diana nodded, warming to her grandmother's logic.

Tim took the dish from her hands as Louisa held the phone out to her.

"Hello."

"Hello, Diana," Marcel's rich voice filtered through the line. "I hope I didn't interrupt anything."

She closed her eyes and tried to control those damn butterflies fluttering in her stomach. "We were just sitting down to dinner."

"Then I apologize and I'll make it brief. I had to move your office temporarily. I had a little accident a few weeks back and broke my ankle."

Diana gasped and then looked around. All eyes were on her. "Are you okay?"

"Fine, fine. It's funny really. I'll have to tell you about it some time. Anyway, we'll work out of my house for a little while."

She stiffened. "What was that?"

"I know it's an inconvenience, but it's the best I can do. I had your desk and belongings moved into the office downstairs. So we're all set."

Diana was speechless. She was going to have to work alone with him in his house?

"And don't worry about Brandy. I'll make sure that she stays out of your way."

She still couldn't think of anything to say.

"So, I guess I'll see you tomorrow then?" Marcel asked.

"Uh, yes. Tomorrow," she managed to say as her mind raced.

"It'll be good seeing you again, Di. Good night."

"Night." She hung up and then looked at her audience. "I'm in trouble."

Eight o'clock the next morning, Diana parked and stared up at Marcel's home. "You can do this," she encouraged herself. "It's just thirty days and then you're out of here." She grabbed her purse and satchel and got out of the car.

When she reached the door, she wasn't sure whether she was supposed to knock or just enter. After a quick internal debate, she rang the bell and then entered.

"Hello?" She glanced around. The rich aroma of coffee drifted out to her and she eased farther inside and closed the door.

To her surprise Brandy raced around the corner and started barking.

Diana immediately dropped everything, but before she could haul butt out of there, a thump upstairs drew her attention. At the loud roar of expletives, she concluded that Marcel needed help.

"Stop barking," she commanded. To her surprise Brandy stopped. "Good girl," she said as an afterthought and then rushed over to the stairs with Brandy trailing behind her. "No. Stay."

Brandy sat.

"Well, what do you know?" she said, amazed.

A few more thumps upstairs caught her attention and she resumed her investigation, but with so many rooms she wasn't sure where she was headed.

"Marcel . . . Mr. Taylor?" Hell, she didn't know what to call him anymore.

"In here," he called out.

She crept down the hallway, unsure which room his voice drifted from. "Where?"

"My bedroom." There were more bumps and then another stream of curses.

How was she supposed to know which room was his bedroom? she wondered wildly. She opened a few wrong doors before she reached the last room in the house. And when she opened it, her breath caught in her throat.

Despite the early morning, there were candles lit in all corners of the room exuding the sweet scent of vanilla.

Pink, yellow, and red rose petals covered every inch of the bedroom floor and a few were sprinkled onto the largest circular bed she'd ever seen. What caught her attention wasn't the rose petals, or the black silk sheets, but the lone high-heeled sandal propped in the center. It was her sandal.

Twenty-six

Marcel emerged from the adjoining bathroom in just his pajama pants and balancing on a pair of crutches. "Looks like you caught me," he said with a weak smile. "I was trying to get things finished before you arrived, but it's a little difficult getting around on these things."

"What's going on?" she asked, inching backward. Her eyes fell to his bare chest and her hand ached to touch him. Droplets of water clung to his hair, signifying that he'd just stepped out of the shower.

"Oh, you mean this?" He looked at the bed. "Do you like it?"

Stunned, she glanced back at the bed and then at him again. "Mr. Taylor, I don't know what you expect me to say and I don't think that it's appropriate for me to be in here." She turned away.

"You're probably right," Marcel said. "I'm just nervous."

She stopped and cast a sideways glance at him. "About what?"

"About this woman I met at the masquerade party." He flashed her a smile. "She's coming over here tonight."

She straightened. "What?"

"Yeah, I know. I didn't want to go to the damn thing, but I'm so glad Solomon talked me into it." He hobbled over to the bed and sat down. "We had this crazy arrangement that he would find me a wife at the ball. I know a person shouldn't just randomly select someone. The institution of marriage shouldn't be taken so lightly. But, it happened."

She watched him with guarded eyes. "What happened?"

He met her steady gaze. "I fell in love."

The declaration shocked her and even caused her to take another step back. "Just like that?"

His smile widened as his gaze lowered to caress her body. "No, it's a little more complicated than that."

"I see."

His intense stare returned to hers. "Do you?"

He knows. That's ridiculous, he couldn't possibly.

Marcel reached for the sandal. "It was a magical night. It was even kind of cute how she selected a Spanish name but spoke with a French accent." He chuckled.

Diana dropped her gaze as a rush of embarrassment coursed through her. Why hadn't she realized that?

"You know, it was kind of her fault how I broke my ankle."

"How?" she asked indignantly.

He smiled. "Well, I guess I can tell you since we're friends and all." He dangled the shoe from his fingers. "My future wife—"

"Your what?"

"Yeah, it's amazing, isn't it? Casanova Brown retiring at last." He struggled to the nightstand and withdrew a jeweler's box. "Do you want to see the ring?"

Curious, Diana floated over to him.

He opened the box and a magnificent emerald-cut diamond gleamed back at her.

"It's beautiful." She sat down on the bed.

"Do you think that she'll like it?"

She pulled her head up to meet his gaze. "Any woman would love this."

He smiled and picked up a small black book from off the table. "I guess it's time to do away with this thing as well." He stood and then used one of his crutches to make it over to the fireplace and tossed the book in.

Diana's eyes bulged. "You're serious."

"I've never been more serious about anything in my entire life."

Diana swallowed.

"Of course I don't know how she feels about me, but I'm determined to find out."

She snapped out of her reverie. "What do you mean?"

He shrugged. "Well, that glorious night ended on the wrong note. Believe it or not she took off before she told me her real name—and with my clothes."

"I'm sorry . . . to hear that." She cleared her throat.

Marcel smiled. "Not as sorry as I was. There I was, left in a bedroom with just my underwear and my shoes and, of course, one of hers."

"So what did you do?"

"Scramble around like a pervert until I found Willy's bedroom. I found some clothes that didn't fit and tried to escape by the back balcony, but I fell off and broke my ankle."

Diana gasped and covered her mouth with her hand. Mostly because she nearly broke her own neck doing the same thing. "That's horrible."

"Yeah." He returned to the bed. "But it'll all be worth it when she walks through that door."

"But you don't know who she is."

Marcel shrugged but held on to his sly smile. "There are clues." He returned to the bed and picked up her shoe. "Solomon suggested that I have all the women invited to the party try this on." He held out the shoe.

She swallowed her rising panic.

He shrugged. "Maybe it only works in fairy tales. There're a lot of holes in that plan. Don't you think?"

Diana nodded, and then jumped when something cold and wet touched her hand.

Brandy barked and smiled up at her.

"I'm sorry, I was supposed to put her out before you arrived."

Diana relaxed and shook her head. "No. She's fine."

Brandy licked her hand again.

"I think she likes you." Marcel leaned over to scratch behind Brandy's ears.

"I like her, too." Diana smiled at the dog.

"Brandy, go downstairs," he instructed.

Brandy obeyed.

"Mind if I ask if you're a good cook?"

"What?" Diana glanced over at him and was surprised to find him sitting so close. The clean scent of soap mingled seductively with his aftershave. Her eyes fell to his lips and desire stirred within her. She wanted to kiss him and lose herself in his arms again. "You still haven't told me how you were going to find this mysterious woman."

"I'm going to use good old-fashioned male intuition."

"Come again?"

He shrugged. "And if that doesn't work, I guess there's always Castleman."

Had someone turned off the air conditioner? She felt hot. "You're going to call Castleman?"

"Actually, I already have. He delivered a folder for me, but I decided not to read it. I want the woman I love to tell me everything. About her parents, how she grew up, her fears, and the things she loves."

Her gaze met his again.

"I'm going to tell her that I've loved her since the moment I laid eyes on her. I loved her before I realized it was love."

"But you don't know what she looks like."

"Sure I do. She's about your height, your weight. Plus, she has this one adorable feature."

"She does?"

"Yeah." He lowered his voice. "Her nose is just slightly off-centered . . . sort of like yours." He tapped the tip of her nose.

Diana couldn't breathe.

He leaned in close and inhaled. "Her skin even smells like yours."

"I—it's a popular fragrance."

"It's my favorite." His beautiful smile returned. "You know, a wise woman once said that a life full of regrets—"

"Is no life at all," she finished for him. A tear trickled down her face.

"I want to hold her in my arms, feel her heart beat against my chest, and taste *your* sweet lips again." He gently wiped away the lone tear.

A small gasp escaped her, but he caught it in a kiss.

Diana melted beneath his sweltering passion. A part of her couldn't believe this was happening. The other part just wanted to enjoy the moment.

When their lips finally broke away, she slid her hand gently down his face. "How long did you know?"

"I told you. The moment I laid eyes on you."

"But why didn't you say something?"

"I was enjoying the game—the mystery. Plus, if it wasn't for that party, God knows how long it would've taken me to realize I loved you. We could've been playing boss and secretary forever."

She glanced down.

"Or until you turned in your resignation."

She kept her eyes lowered. "I was planning to turn it in today."

Marcel's hands fell to his sides. "You know, while I've been spouting words of love, you haven't said anything. How do you feel about me, Diana?"

Her vision blurred as her heart pounded wildly in her chest. "I've been trying to talk myself out of loving you for two years." Tears poured from her eyes. "And it hasn't worked yet."

"I'm glad." Marcel reached for her. "I'm so very

glad." His lips landed gently against hers as his hands caressed her face.

Diana pushed his hands away and gave back his ring. This was going way too fast and made very little sense.

"What's wrong?"

She shook her head as she stood from the bed. "We are. This whole thing. We're two different people. No way a relationship could work between us."

Marcel rubbed at the wrinkles in his forehead and set the jewelry box on the nightstand. "I don't understand. You just said that you loved me."

"I do," she said, pressing a hand against her chest, "but that doesn't mean it's enough." She was just as amazed by the words streaming from her mouth as he was. "You're famous for having a roaming eye."

"That's all behind me." He stood and reached for her hand. "I want you. I've never been more sure of anything in my entire life."

She held his gaze as her heart pounded wildly in her chest. "You don't know anything about me."

"I love what I do know." He gently pulled her closer. "And I intend to spend the rest of my life learning everything that has made you into the beautiful woman you are."

"And Nora?"

He laughed. "There has never been anything between Ms. Gibson and me. In fact, she's no longer an employee at the company."

Diana frowned.

"A couple of days after the ball, she turned in her notice." Marcel shrugged as he frowned. "She did say something weird. She told me to congratulate you—but I have no idea why."

Did Nora know she was Mayte? Probably did since Diana hadn't even been able to fool Marcel.

He cupped her chin with his fingers and forced their gazes to meet. "So what do you say? Will you try on the magic sandal and give us a shot to live happily ever after?"

"I'm scared," she admitted. "People I love always seem to leave me." Louisa's soft smile crossed her mind. "Or are going to leave me."

"I'm not going anywhere, Di. In fact, I'm really praying that you don't walk out of this room right now."

Diana took a deep breath, too scared to believe his words. But how could she walk away from everything she'd ever wanted?

Marcel leaned in and lightly kissed her lips. He pulled the band from her hair. He watched it tumble and settle on her shoulders. "No regrets," he whispered.

She nodded as hot tears spilled over her lashes.

"I love you," he said.

She stared at him through blurred vision. "I love you too."

His mouth lowered against the soft lips. She went weak in his arms as she kissed him just as thoroughly. In no time her heartbeat quickened; her arms and legs tingled. The magic was back.

Diana clung to him, unable to hold anything back as they tumbled onto the bed of rose petals.

Marcel winced at the pain in his ankle, but he uttered no complaint. He was too busy relieving Diana of her clothes. Drunk from the sweet nectar of her lips, he ached to feel her naked form beneath him once again.

Rolling her onto her back, he covered her with

his body, and continued to kiss her as though his life depended on it. He was never going to let her go.

She wrapped her arms around his neck and held him close, but her hold loosened when his soft hands roamed her body.

Marcel didn't want to stop kissing her long enough to get undressed, especially with his cast, but Diana pitched in and his pajama pants were removed with little difficulty.

Tears seeped from Diana's eyes. She never thought this moment would ever come again. And she was thankful that it had.

Sweet words of love tumbled from the lovers' lips as they savored the moment. This time, when they made love it was without games, pretenses, or masks.

They took their time giving and receiving oral pleasure. For Diana, it was all she could do not to crawl up the walls from his unrelenting mouth. Her orgasm slammed into her and caused small waves of aftershock to ripple clear down to her toes.

When her lips claimed his straining flesh, Marcel moaned her name repeatedly. He raked his hands through her hair as his hips surged forward.

"I need you now," he groaned. "Now, Di."

Diana pulled away. "Do you have any condoms?"

Panting, Marcel struggled to reach the nightstand.

"I'll get it." She opened the drawer and quickly found what she was looking for. She took her time sliding the condom down his hard shaft and torturing him at the same time.

"You're killing me," he panted.

She giggled and kissed him as she climbed on top.

She eased down onto his hard shaft and thought that she would die from the sheer pleasure of it.

Marcel groaned as her sleek walls gloved him so hot and tight that he felt as if he were unraveling.

The tempo of their lovemaking started off slow and tender, but quickly escalated to something more hungry and primal.

His ankle be damned. He took over as the aggressor and secured her beneath him. He gladly gave all of himself—something he'd never done before. This was beyond lovemaking. It was the mating of souls.

After a long session, a fire ignited in the center of her and grew into a raging inferno. When her explosive release came at last, her body splintered. A part of her soared into the heavens while the other languished in the arms of her true love.

Marcel's control shattered as his handsome face contorted with pleasure and he emitted a low growl of release.

As their steady heart rhythms mated with their languorous breathing, Diana pressed her cheek against his chest and listened to his heartbeat.

"Di?"

"Hmm?"

"I forgot to do something."

Puzzled, she looked up. "What?"

Gently, he rolled away from her

"Where are you going?"

At the edge of the bed, he took his time lowering to his knees before reaching for the jewelry box from the nightstand.

Diana gasped and drew the silk sheets around her.

"I want to make this official." He opened the box. "Diana Guy, will you marry me?"

She glanced once again at the beautiful diamond and then looked back into his loving face. "Yes!" She scooted to the edge of the bed and then threw her arms around his neck.

He sealed the deal with a kiss. But before he climbed back into bed, he remembered one more thing. He looked around and found the high-heeled sandal on the floor.

"To complete the fantasy."

Diana smiled and presented her right foot.

Marcel slipped the sandal onto her foot. "A perfect fit," he murmured, climbing back onto the bed.

"Now what?" she asked, snuggling beside him.

"We live happily ever after. What else?" He kissed her. "This is forever, sweetheart."

"Yes," Diana answered with a passion that matched his own and once again gave in to the pleasure that only he could give. Now and forever.

Epilogue

the wedding day

On a beautiful June day, Marcel and Diana took their vows before God, friends, and family. It was a nontraditional wedding where Brandy served as the ring bearer, Tim stood as the maid of honor—in a tux—and Ophelia took her place as a groomsman.

After the priest introduced Mr. and Mrs. Marcel Taylor to the guests, a shower of rose petals descended on the smiling couple.

Louisa Mae couldn't stop crying and now demanded that the couple get busy producing babies. Despite feeling the best she'd ever felt, Louisa no longer had an excuse not to visit her doctors. Everyone was amazed and ecstatic to learn that her cancer had gone into remission.

Donald and Camille said their congratulations to the couple and also pressured them about grandchildren.

Marcel was happy to see his parents back together and even enjoyed this new playful side of his father. Maybe the old edict "you don't know what you have until it's gone" was true. With a little luck and a lot of prayer, Marcel would never have to learn that lesson.

At the reception, Solomon approached Ophelia for a dance. He wasn't too happy that she brought a date to the wedding, but hey, it wasn't like he had any right to be jealous. It wasn't the prom, but there was nothing wrong with pretending that it was.

"I'm glad you told me about their love story," Ophelia said, gleaming over at the couple. They look so happy."

"I have a feeling they are." He drew in a deep breath. "Ophelia, there's something I've been dying to tell you."

"There's something I have to tell you too," she said, smiling.

"Oh?"

"Yeah, I told Jonas about Marcel and Diana—"

"Who?"

"My date—Jonas Hinton." She frowned. "You never pay attention to me, do you?"

"Of course I do." He tried to cover up with a smile.

"Well, anyway, Jonas and I have been dating for a while and last night he popped the question."

Solomon's heart dropped. "What question?"

Ophelia slapped him on the shoulder. "*The* question, silly. Now, we haven't picked out a ring, but . . . we're getting married." She bounced excitedly against him. "Isn't that great?"

He stopped dancing. "What?"

Her smile started to ebb away. "Aren't you happy for me?"

Slowly, he managed a butterfly smile. "That's great."

"I know it's a shock." She giggled. "But don't tell Marcel and Diana. I don't want to take anything away from their day."

"My lips are sealed."

She leaned in and kissed his cheek. "Thanks. You know, I want you and Marcel to serve as bridesmaids."

He managed a chuckle. "I wouldn't miss that for the world."

He managed to finish the dance with some semblance of dignity, but soon found himself at the bar.

"What's with the long face?" Marcel asked, slapping him on the back as he joined him. "No one should be frowning on my wedding day."

"Don't worry about me, man. I'm fine. Congratulations again." He looked around. "Where's Diana?"

"Upstairs changing. It's about that time we leave you guys for our honeymoon in Bermuda."

"Ah, white sands and pastel buildings."

"Paradise for thirty days."

"I'm jealous."

"Shouldn't be." He draped an arm around Solomon's shoulder. "I see Ophelia showed up with Jonas."

"Yeah. Don't remind me."

"You know, you better get in there before he snatches up your girl. A woman can only wait for so long."

"You've been married an hour and already you've turned into Dear Abby."

Marcel held up his hands. "Just trying to help you out."

Solomon nodded and glanced back at the dance floor to see Ophelia floating in Jonas's arms.

Minutes later, Diana appeared at the top of the stairs dressed in an all-white linen suit. Below her, a small crowd of single women gathered around for the tossing of the bride's bouquet.

The crowd gasped when an unladylike shove awarded Nora Gibson instead of Marcel's thirteen-year-old cousin with the prize.

"I got it. I got it."

"You sure did, honey." Willy Bassett's smile beamed at her as she slinked next to him.

"Now that's a crazy match," Marcel whispered to Diana.

Seconds later, Solomon won the garter belt toss. He gave Ophelia a long meaningful glance and then held it up for a loud cheer from the crowd.

More rose petals rained down on Marcel and Diana as they made their mad dash to the limo. They stopped briefly so that they both could kiss Louisa's glowing face.

"You make sure that you call us if you need anything."

"I'll be fine. Tim and Caleb are going to stay with me and Brandy in this big house while you're gone."

"I love you, Nana." Diana kissed her again.

"I love you too. Now go and make us some babies."

Marcel and Diana laughed, and continued on their way to the limo.

Inside, Marcel pulled her close for a long kiss. "Are you happy?"

"More than I ever thought possible. Are you?"

He glanced down at her beloved high-heeled sandals. "Who wouldn't be with his own real-life Cinderella?"

She smiled and kissed him again. "Good. I'm going to make sure you stay that way."

AUTHOR'S NOTE

I hope you enjoyed reading *Unforgettable*. Marcel and Diana were a fun couple to write about. Who doesn't like a Cinderella story? Through Louisa I learned a lot about living in the moment and having as few regrets as possible and through Donald and Camille's story I learned a brief lesson about appreciating the people who come into your life. It's easy to take things and people for granted, but I do encourage you to take the time and tell your loved ones exactly what they mean to you. And as for Solomon and Ophelia... I have a feeling there's a lesson to be learned just around the corner.

Best of love,

Adrianne

Adrianne Byrd

Enter the Arabesque 10th Anniversary Contest!

GRAND PRIZE: 1 Winner will receive:
- $10,000 Prize Package

FIRST PRIZE: 5 Winners will receive:
- Special 10th Anniversary limited edition gift
- 1 Year Arabesque Bookclub subscription

SECOND PRIZE: 10 Winners will receive:
- Special 10th Anniversary prize packs

ARABESQUE 10TH ANNIVERSARY CONTEST RULES:

- Contest open January 1–April 30, 2004.
- Mail-In Entries Only (postmarked by 4/30/04 and received by 5/7/04).
- On letter-size paper: Name your favorite Arabesque novel or author and why in 50 words or less.
- Include proof of purchase of an Arabesque novel (send ISBN).
- Include photograph/head shot (4x6 photo preferred, no larger than 5x7).
- Name, address, city, state, zip, daytime phone number and e-mail address.
- Contest entrants must be 21 years of age or older and live in the U.S.
- Only one entry allowed per person.
- Must be able to travel on dates specified: July 30-Aug 1, 2004.
- Send your entry to:

BET Books—10th Anniversary Contest
One BET Plaza
1235 W Street, NE
Washington, DC 20018